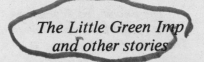

The Little Green Imp and other stories

'Watch!' said his granny. He looked into the bowl, and suddenly out of the green water there jumped a green imp with a potato body and a grinning face! He smacked his hands together and looked up at Twinkle's grandmother.

'You'll do!' said the old lady, and she laughed. Twinkle thanked his grandmother and put the green imp into his pocket. The imp laughed out loud and pinched him once or twice, but Twinkle didn't mind. He guessed that the imp would play a few tricks on Mrs Pudding, the bad-tempered cook!

THE LITTLE GREEN IMP

and other stories

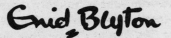

Enid Blyton

Illustrated by Peter Dennis

Beaver Books

A Beaver Book

Published by Arrow Books Limited
62-65 Chandos Place, London WC2N 4NW

An imprint of Century Hutchinson Ltd

London Melbourne Sydney Auckland
Johannesburg and agencies throughout the world

First published in *Mr Icy-Cold,*
Enid Blyton's Annual and *The Grandpa Clock*
Beaver edition 1984
Reprinted 1988

Set in Linoterm Times by JH Graphics Ltd, Reading
Printed and bound in Great Britain
by Anchor Brendon Ltd, Tiptree, Essex

ISBN 0 09 938940 1

Contents

1

Chinky goes adventuring

Chinky was a big, strong brownie who lived in a fine cottage in the middle of Pitpat Village. He had a little friend, a gnome called Dimity, a quiet fellow with a nice smile and neat ways. Dimity thought Chinky a fine brownie and waited on him all day long.

Now Chinky had great ideas of himself. He felt that he had the makings of a hero. If only something would happen so that he could show all the village folk how brave, how full of courage and pluck he was!

'You know, Dimity,' Chinky sometimes said, 'if a house got on fire, I'd be the first one to go and save all the people in it!'

'I'm sure you would, Chinky,' said Dimity admiringly.

'And if a horse ran away I'd be the first one to stop him!' said Chinky.

'There's no doubt about that!' said Dimity, gazing in admiration at tall, strong Chinky.

'And if someone fell into the pond and

couldn't swim I'd jump in straight away and pull him out!' boasted Chinky.

'But I thought you couldn't swim,' said Dimity.

'Oh, that wouldn't matter!' said Chinky. 'I'd be brave enough to jump in all the same.'

'You are so big and strong, Chinky,' said Dimity, with a sigh. 'I'm such a little fellow, and not brave at all. Why, I even run when I see a big spider!'

'You are weak and foolish, Dimity,' said Chinky grandly. 'Never mind – you have a brave friend. If only I could show what a fine chap I am! Nobody seems to think I am anything out of the ordinary. I never have any adventures.'

It was true. Pitpat Village was quiet and well-behaved. No one did anything they shouldn't. Nobody ever had a house on fire. None of the horses ever ran away. Nobody ever fell into the pond or the stream. There were no adventures to be had at all.

So no one knew that Chinky felt so brave. They just nodded to him when they met him, and said 'Good-day!' Or they asked him out to tea and showed him their fine roses or their best sweet-peas and their biggest marrows. It seemed very dull to big, brave Chinky.

'Dimity,' said Chinky, at last, 'I am going to seek adventures. Pack up our things and we

8

will set out tomorrow. If adventures will not come to me, I must go to them.'

So Dimity packed their things into one big bag, put it on his shoulder and set out with his friend. Chinky had long, strong legs and he got along fast. Dimity was always out of breath, for his legs were thin and small, and he had to carry the heavy bag. So he always seemed to be running to catch up.

They walked and they walked. They passed right through Pitpat Village and Chinky shouted to everyone how he was going on brave adventures, and they nodded in surprise.

'You will do something one day, Chinky!' they called, and Chinky marched on, pleased. He left the village behind. He came to farm land, and walked over fields and meadows. And then he came to his first adventure!

'Look!' he cried, stopping and pointing, 'there is something on fire!'

Dimity looked. Yes – smoke was rising up from behind a hedge, and flames crackled loudly.

'It must be a shed or something,' said Chinky. 'Hurry, Dimity, and get a pail for me. There is a stream here, and I will put out the fire. I knew I could be a hero if I had the chance!'

Dimity rushed to a barn not far off, found a

pail, and took it to Chinky. Chinky filled it with water from the stream and threw it on the fire. He got more water and threw it on the flames – and yet more. Soon the fire sizzled loudly, and a cloud of black smoke rose into the air instead of flames and blue smoke.

'The fire is going out,' said Chinky. 'I have put it out!'

Just at that moment there came a roar from behind him. Chinky turned and saw a farmer standing there looking very angry indeed.

'What have you done to my bonfire?' he shouted. 'I was burning up all my rubbish – and now you have interfered and put out the fire! You deserve a good whacking!'

Chinky stared at the angry farmer and then at the fire. Yes – it was a bonfire. He could see that quite plainly now. The farmer lifted up his stick and ran towards Chinky – and the brownie ran away in a terrible fright! Over the fields he ran, and up the hill and down, and he didn't stop till he had lost all his breath. Dimity panted behind him.

Chinky said nothing at all. He didn't feel very brave. Soon he got up and went on again, and it wasn't long before he found his next adventure!

'Look!' he said to Dimity. 'Someone has left their shopping basket behind! They must have put it down for a moment and then forgotten it.

10

We will find the owner – and how pleased she will be!'

Dimity saw the basket by the hedge, full of bags and parcels. Yes – someone had been shopping – but who? There was no one in sight.

'Shall I carry the basket, Chinky?' Dimity asked.

'Oh, no, I'll carry it,' said Chinky, who was longing to see the owner and have her thanks. He picked it up and set off with it. But he hadn't gone very far before there came an angry yell from the other side of the hedge.

'Stop thief! Stop thief! He's got my basket! I just stepped through the hedge to say good morning to Mrs Flip and someone came along and took my basket! There's the thief! Stop thief! Stop thief!'

A big fat brownie woman came running down the path, red in the face, looking as angry as could be. Behind her came another brownie woman, carrying a rolling-pin.

'Excuse me, madam,' began Chinky politely – but the brownie women did not listen to him. One smacked him on the cheek and the other hit him on the shoulder with her rolling-pin. Poor Chinky! He dropped the basket and fled down the path as fast as ever he could, crying tears all down his nice new coat! He was dreadfully frightened.

Dimity followed with the big bag, panting and puffing, very sorry for his friend.

Chinky dried his tears and went on his way. He felt brave again, ready to go in for any adventure that came, but he did not mean to put out fires nor to pick up baskets. No – he wanted something grander than that!

And he soon found it! He came to a river and saw, in the middle, a boat, rowed by a magician. Sitting in the boat were four pixie-like creatures, with no wings. Just as the boat floated opposite, the magician stopped rowing, took hold of the first pixie and threw him into the water!

'One!' he said. Then he took the second and threw him in as well, 'Two!' Then the third – 'Three!' And then the last. 'Four!' shouted the magician, and stood up in his boat shouting in excitement.

'Look!' said Chinky to Dimity, throwing off his coat. 'Four poor little pixies thrown into the water by that wicked magician! I must rescue them!'

'But you can't swim!' wailed Dimity. Chinky took no notice. He dived into the water and tried to wade out to the pixies – but the water was deep, and, as Dimity had said, Chinky could not swim! So he began to flounder about and shout for help at the top of his voice.

The four pixies, who had been swimming very strongly to the opposite bank, turned at once and made their way to the struggling brownie. They surrounded him and took him to the boat. The magician pulled him in and gazed angrily at him.

'What do you want to get into deep water like this for when you can't swim?' he said. 'I put my four pixies in to have a race, and you have spoilt it all. Silly, interfering creature! I shall take you back with me and make you my servant! Spoiling my plans like this!'

Chinky was dreadfully frightened. He didn't say a word. He didn't like to tell the magician that he had thought he was cruel and had thrown the pixies into the water to drown them. He sat in the boat, shivering and trembling.

Dimity was on the bank, in a terrible way, wondering what was going to happen to Chinky. As the boat was rowed along, he followed it, running on the path. Soon the boat pulled up at a landing-stage, and Dimity saw the magician take hold of poor Chinky very roughly, and haul him up a path and into his house. The four pixies followed. The door slammed. Chinky was a prisoner!

Dimity sat down in dismay. He was very much afraid of magicians. But somehow or other Chinky had got to be rescued. He waited until night had come and everything was dark. Then he crept round to the back of the house and looked in at the window. There, sitting in a corner, with his hands tied, he saw Chinky. No one was with him. Good!

Dimity broke the window with a stone, jumped inside, cut the cords that bound Chinky's hands, and pulled him to the window. At that moment the magician came running in – but Dimity picked up a chair and threw it at him. The magician fell over and yelled in surprise. Before he had picked himself up Chinky and Dimity had disappeared into the night!

And it wasn't *very* long before the two of them were sitting safely and comfortably at home, drinking hot cocoa and grinning shyly at one another. Chinky looked rather red.

'Dimity,' he said, 'I have been foolish. I have found that I am not a hero after all. I don't want to be one, either. I want to stay happily at home with you. But you, Dimity, you are a *real* hero! When I was caught and tied up by the magician, you rescued me, though you must have been very much afraid. You are a brave fellow, Dimity, full of courage. I am proud to have you for a friend!'

Dimity was too happy to speak at first. Then he hugged Chinky and smiled. 'I'm not a hero!' he said. 'I don't want to be one, either. But I love you, Chinky, and so I was brave. But I am not brave really!'

So they had no more adventures, which was just as well, and lived happily together in Pitpat Village – and, unless they have moved, they are still there, to this very day!

2

The Grandpa clock

The Grandpa clock stood up on the landing all day and night, ticking solemnly away by himself. He was a very tall clock, much, much taller than the children, and he was really a grandfather clock, of course – but everyone called him Grandpa because he was so nice.

He didn't like being up on the bedroom landing. He wanted to be down in the hall, and see a bit of life. He wasn't even on the front landing – he was on the back one, where the box room and the guest-room were, so he didn't really see much of anything that went on in the house.

'I wish I was down in the hall!' he thought whenever he heard someone ringing the bell or knocking at the door. 'I wonder who that is? Why can't I be down there and see? And I wish I could go and visit the kitchen. So many people come there. I can hear their voices. The cat goes there a lot too, and I like her.'

But it wasn't a bit of good, the back landing

was his place and there he had to stay. Until one exciting day came – and then things were suddenly quite different!

It happened one night that a small imp called Scuttle-About lost his way in the dark, and climbed in at the landing window to take shelter. He heard the tick-tock, tick-tock of the Grandpa clock, and he ran to it.

'Can I get inside you?' he whispered. 'Will you hide me, Grandpa Clock?'

'Yes! I've a door under my big face. Open it and creep inside,' said Grandpa. 'Be careful of my pendulum that swings to and fro, though. It might hit you.'

The imp was very careful of it. He crouched down below it, and felt it just scrape the top of his head as it swung to and fro. Tick-tock, tick-tock!

He took off his Scuttle-About shoes. They were very magic and he could run about fast as a hare in them – but his feet were tired now and he wanted to curl up and rest for the night.

Soon he was fast asleep and snoring a little. Grandpa ticked steadily all the time, feeling most excited to have a little imp asleep just under his pendulum!

'Tick-tock! It's time to be up! Tick-tock! You must hurry away!' ticked old Grandpa, when he heard the birds beginning to sing outside. He knew that Annie the cook would soon be up and about. He didn't want her to see the imp when he ran off again.

Scuttle-About woke up with a jump. He stretched himself and hit the swinging pendulum with his hand.

'Hey, don't do that!' said Grandpa. 'You'll make me go slow! Hurry – I believe I can hear someone coming.'

The imp swung open the door and fled in a fright. Grandpa never saw him again. But Scuttle-About left something behind him – he left his little magic shoes!

And soon the magic in them spread to the old Grandpa clock. He suddenly felt restless. He ticked a little faster. And then, to his enormous surprise, he gave a little jiggety-jig, rocking to and fro as he ticked.

'Strange! I seem to be able to move!' said Grandpa, astonished. 'I'm sure I moved forward a bit then. There! I did it again. Good gracious – I've moved out from the wall!'

It was the Scuttle-About spell in the little shoes working, of course. But Grandpa didn't know that. He just thought that for some strange reason he could move about.

Move about! Why, he had always longed to do that. He had always wanted to go into the hall and into the kitchen. Suppose he could? Just suppose he could get himself downstairs – how exciting that would be!

Well, it was difficult for him to move very much at first, but he soon got used to it. He could only move by rocking himself, or doing a curious little jump that made him tick very fast indeed as if he were quite out of breath.

It took him quite half an hour to reach the front landing. Even that was exciting to him because it was years since he had seen it. There were flowers there, and a big chair, and a chest. Grandpa ticked away to them in a loud voice: 'I'm going downstairs when I've got my breath! I'm going exploring!'

But he didn't get downstairs because at that moment the children's father came out of his room to go and wake the children. He almost bumped into Grandpa, who was just outside his bedroom door.

'Good gracious! It's the Grandpa clock!' he said. 'However did it get here? Has someone been having a joke?'

Poor Grandpa! He was carried straight back to his own place on the back landing. He was bitterly disappointed. He grumbled away to himself, ticking very crossly.

'Tick-tock, what a nasty shock, for a poor old clock!' he ticked. The children soon heard that he had been found outside their father's door, and they came to stare at him.

'Who put you there? Grandpa, don't you start wandering about at night!' they said.

Well, the Grandpa clock wasn't going to stop his bit of travelling if he could help it! Somehow or other he was going to get downstairs! Surely, if the family found him in the hall they would let him stay there? Wasn't that the proper place for a big grandfather clock?

That afternoon, when the children were at school and their mother was resting, the clock felt it couldn't keep still on the dull back landing any longer. He must at least go to the top of the stairs and look down.

So he went to the top of the stairs, rocking himself slowly along, sometimes giving a funny little jump. He couldn't help feeling very excited.

The stairs looked very long and very steep. It wasn't much good thinking of rocking himself down them. He would have to do jumps down from one stair to the next. Down he went – jump – jump – jump – hop!

It was very dangerous. He nearly missed a stair once or twice, and shivered in fright. But at last he was at the bottom, standing in the hall. How wonderful!

The hall seemed a most exciting place. There were mats and chairs, umbrellas, walking-sticks and a little table with flowers on. Now, where could the clock put himself so that he could see when people came to the door? He badly wanted to have a bit of company.

The cat had heard the noise Grandpa made coming downstairs, and she came out of the kitchen to see what it was. She was amazed to see the Grandpa clock standing by the hall-table! She went up and sniffed at it. The sniffing tickled Grandpa, and made him jump.

That frightened the cat. She put her tail in the air and fled to the kitchen. The clock heard voices coming from there.

'I must go there and listen,' he thought, so he rocked and hopped to the kitchen door. The cook was out in the scullery talking to the milkman and the baker. Grandpa rocked inside and stood by the cupboard. My, what a thrilling place the kitchen was – and look at that lovely red fire! Grandpa began to wish he lived in the kitchen.

The cook came back. She saw Grandpa at once and gave a scream. 'Milkman! Baker! Help, help! Here's old Grandpa in the kitchen!'

They came rushing in, expecting to see an old man. Cook pointed to the clock. 'There, look! How did he get here? Oh, oh, I feel faint!'

The Grandpa clock was scared. When the milkman and the baker helped the cook to a chair, he rocked himself out of the kitchen and put himself back in the hall. He stood there, feeling very excited. My word, this was life!

The children's mother came running down the stairs. She suddenly saw Grandpa by the hall table, and stopped in amazement.

'Cook!' she called. 'Why is Grandpa down in the hall!'

'Oh, Mam! Do you mean to say he's there now?' cried the cook, looking into the hall. 'He was standing in the kitchen a minute ago!'

'Oh, nonsense!' said the children's mother. *How* did he get into the hall? This is most extraordinary.'

The children were surprised to hear what had happened when they got home.

The cook told them how Grandpa had appeared in the kitchen, then their mother told them how she had seen him in the hall.

'Perhaps old Grandpa is dull and bored, living up on the back landing, where nothing happens and nobody goes,' said Mary. 'Can't we let him live in the hall? He's so nice.'

But back on the landing he had to go. He was really most annoyed. Now he would have to hop all the way downstairs again if he wanted to stand in the hall.

'I'll wait till night comes and everyone is in bed,' he thought, ticking solemnly on the landing. 'Then I'll go down again, and look into all the rooms. That will be most exciting.'

Now, that night, when it was very dark and everyone was asleep, old Grandpa thought he

22

would go downstairs once more. And at the same moment that he thought this he heard a little noise downstairs. Who was it? The cat wandering about? Or mice playing? Perhaps it was that imp coming back again.

Grandpa decided to go and see. So off he went, rocking himself to the top of the stairs. He stood at the top, and heard a noise again. The noise wasn't the cat, or the mice, or the imp. It was a burglar! He had got into the house and was in the hall. Think of that!

Grandpa hopped down the first stair. Then he hopped down the next one – but alas, he missed! With a really tremendous noise he slid and slithered all the way from the top to the bottom, and landed on the top of the alarmed burglar. He was knocked over like a skittle, and lay on the carpet, quite still.

Then things happened quickly. Doors flew open, lights went on, voices called out. 'What was that noise, what's happening?' And down the stairs poured the whole family.

'Why, my goodness me, here's a man lying flat on the floor and the old Grandpa clock on top of him!' said the children's father in astonishment. 'Ring up the police, quickly!'

The police came. They took the burglar away. One of them nodded at the old clock, which had now been stood upright in the hall,

and was watching everything in the greatest excitement.

'What was your clock doing, knocking burglars down in the middle of the night? Good thing you had him in the hall!'

'Well, we didn't. He lives on the back landing,' said Mary. 'But oh – do, do let him live downstairs in the hall, Daddy, will you? I'm sure he wants to! I'm sure he was coming downstairs and he slipped and fell on top of the burglar. He deserves a reward, Daddy, he really does!'

So now old Grandpa lives downstairs, and loves it. And nobody has discovered to this day that he has a tiny pair of Scuttle-About shoes inside his case! It will be sad if somebody takes them out, won't it? He won't ever be able to wander into the kitchen at night and talk to the cat.

Tick-tock, tick-tock. I believe I can hear him coming!

3

Mister Icy-Cold

Once upon a time, one very snowy week, six children began to build a snowman. How hard they worked! You should have seen them, scraping the snow off the grass and off the top of the hedges, slapping it together to make the snowman's body, and patting it neatly into shape.

'This is fun!' said Mary.

'He will be the biggest snowman ever seen!' said Alan.

'I shall ask Mother to give me an old cap of Daddy's for him to wear,' said Eileen.

'Let's give him two feet, and put shoes on them so that he can walk about if he wants to!' said John.

The others laughed. 'I *should* be astonished if I saw him walking down the garden!' said Ian.

'We'll call him Mister Icy-Cold!' said Gillian.

When they had finished the snowman it was

three o'clock. 'Now we will dress him!' said Mary.

'He has a head as big as a giant's football!' said Alan.

'Here's Daddy's old cap for him!' said Eileen, running up with a big checked cap and putting it on the snowman's head. He did look grand!

'And here are two old shoes belonging to Grandpa!' said John, putting them on the snowman's feet. It was difficult to put them on! John filled the shoes with snow, and then pushed them well under the snowman, so that they stuck out in a very real manner!

'He's going to walk, he's going to walk!' cried Ian.

'Come along indoors and have a nice hot drink of milk, Mister Icy-Cold!' shouted Gillian.

'He wouldn't like that,' said Mother, coming up to look at the wonderful snowman. 'It would melt him inside!'

The children went in to tea. When the moon rose up in the sky, just about their bed-time, they looked out of the window and saw Mister Icy-Cold standing out there in the garden looking as real as could be. He wore Daddy's cap, he smoked an old pipe, he had two great black eyes, he wore a ragged scarf round his neck, old gloves on his hands,

27

and Grandpa's shoes. He really looked marvellous.

In the middle of the night a crowd of little snow-elves came flying up in their pretty sleigh, drawn by winter moths. When they saw Mister Icy-Cold they flew down to him at once.

'Oh!' they cried. 'A great big snowman! What is your name, Snowman?'

'I am Mister Icy-Cold,' said the snowman, in a soft snowy sort of voice. 'Come and talk to me.'

The snow-elves told him where they had come from – a land far away to the north, where there was always ice, always frost, always snow. The elves were pretty little creatures with frosty dresses, and wings as soft and as white as snow. Mister Icy-Cold liked them very much indeed. He felt lonely when they had gone. But they promised to come again the next night.

They kept their promise – but to Mister Icy-Cold's great dismay they were crying bitterly!

'What's the matter?' asked Mister Icy-Cold.

'Oh, two naughty pixies chased us, and broke our pretty sleigh. Look! It's no use now! We can't use it any more. We don't know what to do because, when the weather turns warm, we must fly away to our own country of ice and snow. If we stay here when it is warm, we feel ill and fade away.'

Mister Icy-Cold was very sorry to hear all this.

'Where do those two pixies live?' he asked. 'I will go to them and make them mend your sleigh for you, or else give you a new one.'

'But snowmen can't walk!' cried the snow-elves.

'Oh, *can't* they!' said Mister Icy-Cold, and he laughed. 'Look!'

He stepped forward on his two big feet, and the elves cried out in surprise, for they had never seen a snowman walk before. He plodded down the garden and back, his two big shoes leaving footprints behind him.

'There you are!' he said. 'What did I tell you? Now where do those two naughty pixies live? I'll go and give them the fright of their lives!'

'Come with us and we'll show you,' said the elves, and dragging their broken sleigh behind them, they took the snowman down the garden, through a gate at the bottom, and into a field. The field sloped up into a hill, and in the middle of the hill was a little door.

'This is where the pixies live,' said the elves, half-frightened. Mister Icy-Cold knocked at the door softly. As soon as it was opened by the two pixies, the snowman reached out his big gloved hand and caught hold of them.

'Oooh! Ow! Oooh!' yelled the pixies, in a

29

fright. 'He's a big white giant! Oooh! Let us go!'

'You broke the sleigh belonging to the snow-elves!' said the snowman sternly. 'What are you going to do about it?'

'Oh, we'll mend it; oh, do let us go! We promise to mend it!' squealed the pixies. Mister Icy-Cold put them down on the ground, and looked at them sternly out of his big black stone eyes.

'Do it at once, or I'll carry you off with me!' he said. The pixies took the broken sleigh and looked at it. One of them fetched hammer and nails and screws. The other brought a few pieces of wood. Soon the night air was filled with the sound of hammering. Every now and again the two pixies stared round in fear at the big snowman, and he frowned as hard as he could.

'Get on with your job!' he said. So they hurried and hurried. The wind blew chill and Jack Frost was out and about. The pixies were cold and wanted to get back into their warm little house. Soon the sleigh was mended, and the snow-elves got into it with glad shouts and cries.

'Don't you dare to interfere with the snow-elves again,' said Mister Icy-Cold, and off he shuffled back to his place in the garden. The snow-elves went with him, making a great fuss of him, and telling him he was their best friend.

After that the elves and the snowman talked together every night. But soon the weather changed and the air became warm. The snow-elves began to think about going back to their own country of ice and snow.

'But how lonely I shall be without you!' said Mister Icy-Cold sadly. 'I shall stand here, thinking of you, all the spring and summer

through, till the winter comes again and brings you with it.'

'No, Mister Icy-Cold, you won't stay here all the spring and the summer,' said the elves. 'You will melt. You will melt right away, and there will be nothing left of you when we come back next winter.'

Mister Icy-Cold stared at the elves in horror, and his stone eyes seemed to get bigger and bigger.

'Melt!' he said. 'Did you say I shall melt? Won't there be anything left of me?'

'Not a thing,' said the elves sadly. 'That's the worst of being a snowman, you know. You only last whilst the snow and ice are here. Then you disappear for ever.'

Nobody spoke for a minute. Mister Icy-Cold was too upset, and the elves too sad. Then a small elf gave a little squeal that made everybody jump.

'I've got an idea, I've got an idea!' she cried. 'Why shouldn't Mister Icy-Cold come back to our land with us! It's always cold and frosty there, and snow is always on the ground. He would never melt there. He would be able to live with us for ever!'

'Of course, of course!' shouted the snow-elves in delight. 'You must start tonight, Mister Icy-Cold. We will make our winter moths fly very slowly, and you must follow us carefully.

Come now, this very minute – for the weather is getting warmer, and if you begin to melt you may not be able to walk!'

So Mister Icy-Cold followed the little sleigh, drawn by moths, and plodded on and on and on towards the north. He went over fields and hills, down lanes and high roads, and the elves always found a good place to hide him in the daytime.

Once the weather got a bit too warm, and the snowman's nose melted a bit. But the next night was frosty again, so he was all right. And at last he got to the land of the snow-elves. He was safe!

'Welcome to our home!' cried the snow-elves, kissing him on his cold cheek. 'You shall build yourself a little snow-house with windows and a door, and do just whatever you like.'

The six children who had built the snowman were most surprised to find him gone.

'Oh, he's just melted,' said Mother.

'But, Mother, his cap, and his scarf, and his gloves and his shoes can't have melted too!' said Mary. 'It's most mysterious! I wonder where he is, funny old Mister Icy-Cold?'

He was building himself a little house in the land of the snow-elves, as happy as could be! And there he lives to this day, still wearing the same old cap and the same old shoes – funny Mister Icy-Cold!

4

Wisky, Wasky and Weedle

Once upon a time there were three gnomes called Wisky, Wasky and Weedle. Wisky was small, Wasky was tall, and Weedle was fat. They were lazy, mischievous rascals, and they lived in a tiny cottage called Chimneys.

Now one day when Wisky wanted to go out to buy sausages for dinner, he found there was no money at all in the purse they kept on the mantelpiece. He turned it inside out and showed it to the others.

'We've got to do some work, boys,' he said. 'No money, no sausages!'

They sat down on their stools to think hard. Presently Wisky grinned and slapped his knee. 'I've got a fine idea!' he said.

'What?' asked the others.

'We'll borrow Mr Sooty's chimney-brushes,' said Wisky. 'And we'll go to the next town where nobody knows us. I will be the sweep and sweep the chimney; but I'll be sure to make the carpets and everything in a dreadful mess before I go – and that's where *you* come in, Wasky!'

'Go on,' said Wasky.

'You see, as soon as I have left, and the lady is grumbling about the soot all over the place, *you* come up, Wasky, with brooms and dusters and cloths, and say you are a cleaner. So you get the job of going in and cleaning the house.'

'And where do *I* come in?' asked Weedle.

'Well, before Wasky goes, he leaves the taps running,' said naughty Wisky, with a giggle. 'Then, just as the water is running over everywhere and the lady is trying to get a plumber to come in and put things right, *you* come along, Weedle, and say you are a handyman and can do any job like that. You turn off the taps, clear up the mess, take your pay and join us! Now isn't that a fine idea? We each make a job for the other, you see.'

'Come on, then,' said Wasky, getting up. 'You go and borrow Mr Sooty's brushes, Wisky.'

Very soon, with chimney-brushes, ordinary brushes, and dusters and cloths and a bag of tools, the three gnomes went over the hill to Fiddle-dee-dee, the next town. They looked about for a house where the smoke from a chimney was very black, for they knew that perhaps that would want sweeping – and very soon they saw one.

'Look, there's a chimney that wants sweeping!' said Wisky, pointing to it. 'Now I go first, boys.'

Off he went to the back door, carrying his sweep's brushes over his shoulder. He rang the bell. A sharp-faced little brownie-woman came to the door.

'Good morning, madam; your chimney wants sweeping and I'm the man to do it for you,' said Wisky, taking off his cap.

'Are you clean in your work, and quick?' asked the brownie-woman. Wisky said he was – and she led the way indoors and up to a bedroom where a fire was burning. She put it out and told Wisky to sweep the chimney and not make a mess.

Wisky fitted together his chimney-brushes and pushed them up the chimney. He meant to make a fine old mess, of course – but, dear me, he didn't need to try to make one! That chimney was almost choked up with soot, and as soon as Wisky's brush moved it, a great pile of fine black soot fell down the chimney, bounced on the hearth and covered Wisky from top to toe! He began to cough and splutter. The soot flew out into the room and settled everywhere – my, what a mess there was!

Wisky took a look at it. He felt frightened. He hadn't meant to make quite such a mess as

36

that! He stuck his head up the chimney to see if there was any more soot there – and another lot fell all over him!

'I'd better stop this,' thought Wisky. 'I'll put my brushes together and go downstairs and ask for my money. I'm sorry for Wasky! He *will* have a mess to clear up!'

He went downstairs. When the brownie-woman saw him she gave a scream.

'Ooooooh! What are you?'

'I'm the chimney-sweep, madam,' said poor Wisky.

'Well, you want a wash,' said the brownie-woman, and she took hold of Wisky by his hair and popped him just as he was into a tub of hot soapy water she had nearby, ready for her washing. My goodness me! What a shock for Wisky! But that wasn't all. When she had finished washing him she took him out into the garden and pegged him up on the line by his coat-collar to dry. Poor Wisky!

Now Wasky and Weedle were waiting outside, and when Wisky didn't come out, Wasky was cross.

'He's slipped out of the back door with his money and gone home,' said Wasky. 'It's too bad. Well, I'm going in to do my share, Weedle. You'll be next.'

He went and knocked at the door. The brownie-woman opened it, looking worried and upset, for she had just seen the terrible mess in her bedroom.

'Any cleaning you want done, madam?' asked Wasky, showing his brooms and dusters. 'I'm the man for you, if you've got a dirty room you want turned out!'

'Well, it just happens I *do* want someone,' said the brownie-woman. 'I've had a sweep here and he has left the bedroom in such a mess that I really don't know what to do about it. Come in.'

In stepped Wasky and went up to the bedroom, grinning, but when he saw the truly dreadful mess everywhere that Wisky had left, he turned quite pale. What, clean up all that! Good gracious, it would take him hours, and be too much like real hard work! But he had to set to work.

Now Wasky had no real idea how to clean a dirty sooty room, and he set to work to sweep up the soot with his biggest brush – and, of course, the soot flew up into the air and made more mess than ever! Wasky got desperate – he swept and he swept – and the soot flew and flew. It got into his eyes – and his nose – and his mouth – it flew from the bedroom into the bathroom. Wasky made the mess twice as bad, and was quite frightened when he suddenly caught sight of himself in the glass.

'Gracious me!' he said. 'How dreadful I

look! I think I'll just turn on a few taps so that
there is a nice watery mess for Weedle to clear
up – and then I'll ask for my money and go.'

He turned on all the taps he could see. Then
he shut the bathroom door and went downstairs. But before he could even open his
mouth to ask for his money, the brownie-
woman gave a shriek! 'What! You're as bad as
the chimney-sweep!' she cried. 'What a dreadful mess you are in!'

She popped Wasky into a tub of soapy water and soon he too was out on the line, hanging there in the wind beside Wisky! And Weedle waited outside the house, wondering why Wasky didn't come out.

At last he went to the door and rang the bell, just in time to hear the brownie-woman shouting for help.

'Something's gone wrong with the water! The water is pouring down the stairs! Help! Help!'

Weedle went in with his bag of tools. 'Madam, I am a plumber,' he said. 'I will soon put things right for you.'

He rushed upstairs and turned off the taps. My goodness, you should have seen the bathroom! The bath was full and overflowing, and so was the basin. There was water swirling about the floor, running out on to the landing, into the bedroom and down the stairs! What with the black soot everywhere, and the water, there was a fine old muddle!

Suddenly, Weedle slipped and fell – splash! into the water. 'Oooooomph!' he said, as he swallowed a huge mouthful of sooty water. 'Oooooomph! It's down my neck! It's in my boots! It's all over me! Help! Help! I'm drowning! I can't swim!'

He tried to get up but fell over again – and suddenly down the stairs he slid with the pouring water, and landed – ker-plumkity-plunk! – at the bottom. There the brownie-woman stood, with rubber boots on, trying to sweep the water out of the back door.

'Bless us all!' she said, as she caught hold of Weedle by the hair and shook him well. 'Here's another to go on the line.'

And will you believe it, she took Weedle and pegged him up on the line to dry too! There the three gnomes hung in the wind, swinging to and fro, wishing and wishing they had never thought of playing such tricks on anyone!

The brownie-woman swept her house out and dried it. She cleaned away the soot and opened the windows to let the air in. And then she took a carpet-beater and she went to the line where Wisky, Wasky and Weedle hung, and gave them all the hardest spanking they had had in their lives.

'You are three rogues!' she said, as she unpegged them. 'I can see through your tricks. Now go home, and make up your minds to do better – or I'll come and peg you up on my line again, as sure as my name is Dame Slip-Slap.'

Poor Wisky, Wasky and Weedle! I feel sorry for them – but it served them right all the same, didn't it!

5

The cow that lost her moo

There was once a pretty cow called Buttercup. Everyone was very fond of her, for she was a gentle creature, though rather stupid. She lived in a big field with twelve other cows, and she was the prettiest of the lot.

One day she caught a cold and she lost her voice. She tried her hardest to moo loudly just as she had always done – but it wasn't any good at all. Not the tiniest bit of moo came out of her big mouth. Buttercup had no voice except a small whisper that sounded rather like dry leaves rustling together.

'This will never do!' thought Buttercup to herself in a great fright. 'I *must* get some sort of voice. I can't go about whispering. Even the ducks on the pond over there have a louder voice than I have. If I can't moo perhaps I can learn to quack!'

So that night, when the Little Folk came running out in the fields, Buttercup whispered to one of them.

'Pinkity, I've lost my lovely moo. Could you get me another one, do you think? – or at any rate could you get me another voice of some sort? I hate talking in a whisper like this; it is so stupid for a big cow like me to have such a tiny whispery voice.'

Pinkity looked at the great cow and grinned all over his cheeky little face. 'I can't get you a moo,' he said. 'But I could get you a quack, if you like! I know those ducks would spare me one if I asked them.'

Buttercup nodded her head. Off went Pinkity, spoke to the ducks, and then came back with something wrapped up in a dock leaf. 'Here you are,' he said to the grateful cow. 'Swallow this and you'll find you have a fine new voice!'

So Buttercup swallowed down the dock leaf with the quack spell inside – and at once she found that she could quack! You should have heard her! Really, it was very funny to hear a great cow quacking away for all she was worth. Her friends came round her in surprise.

'Why do you quack?' they asked. 'You are very foolish, Buttercup. The farmer will think you are a duck, and will put you on the pond to swim with the others. You will have to lay eggs for him.'

'Quack, quack!' cried Buttercup, in a great fright. 'I couldn't lay an egg! I know I couldn't!

And I should die of fear if I had to swim on the pond! Pinkity, where are you? Quack, quack, quack! Take away this quack and bring me some other voice. I can't bear it!'

Pinkity hopped up. He was very much enjoying himself. He caught a loud quack as Buttercup spoke, and wrapped it up in another dock leaf. He put it into his pocket, and hurried off. He went to a brown mouse for a little squeak. She gave it to him wrapped up in a daisy leaf, for it was very small.

He ran back to Buttercup and gave it to her. She swallowed it – and then began to squeak in a very high voice, just like the mouse. All the other cows began to moo with laughter.

'Buttercup, how foolish you are!' they said. 'Now you have a voice like a mouse. The weasel will come along when he hears you, and will try to bite you, thinking you are a mouse – and the big owl will pounce down on you.'

'Too-whoo-too-whoo!' called the owl, in the distance. Buttercup began to tremble. She was in a great fright.

'Pinkity, Pinkity!' she squeaked. 'Come here! Take away this squeak, I beg of you, and bring me a better voice. I can't bear this. Squeak, squeak. Eeeeeeee!'

Pinkity took away the squeak and ran off again, beaming. This was a great joke. What a tale to tell when he went home in the morning!

44

This time he went to a sheep lying down on the hillside, and asked her to lend him her baa. She did so, and he carried it off, wrapped up in two nettle leaves. Buttercup swallowed it gratefully and at once began to baa and bleat in a most sheep-like manner.

All her friends stared at her in amazement. Whatever would she do next?

'Buttercup, are you turning into a sheep?' asked Daisy, a pretty white cow.

'No,' said Buttercup. 'Of course not. I am a cow. Baa-aa! Baa-aa!'

'Well, the farmer will be sure to think you are a sheep if you baa like that,' said Daisy. 'He will expect you to grow wool for him and will clip your coat just as he does those of the sheep. My! You will be cold with all your coat clipped away!'

Buttercup was horrified. What! Have her nice hairy coat clipped away so that she might grow a thick covering of wool? Never! 'Baa, baa, baa!' she bleated to Pinkity. 'Oh, do take this voice away quickly. I can't bear it. Baa, baa!'

Pinkity hopped up and took it away. He gave it back to the surprised sheep, and then hunted round for someone else who might lend him a voice. He met Bobby, the dog, out rabbiting by himself in the moonlight, and he called to him.

'Hi, Bobby! Will you lend me your bark for a little while?'

'No,' said Bobby. 'I want it.'

'Now, listen, Bobby,' said Pinkity. 'I'll show you the best rabbit-hole in the field if you'll lend me your bark for a time. Please do. I'm having such fun with a foolish cow. I've made her quack, squeak and baa. Now I want to make her bark.'

'Well, mine's a very *fierce* sort of bark,' said Bobby. 'She will frighten all the other cows if they hear it. So I warn you, Pinkity . . . you'd really better not borrow it!'

But Pinkity said yes, he really must have it. So Bobby gave it to him, wrapped up in a piece of paper he found in the ditch. Off went Pinkity over the fields to Buttercup. 'Here you are,' he said, giving her the bark in the piece of paper. She ate it up, paper and all.

And then, stars and moon! She began to bark like a very fierce dog!

'Wuff, wuff, wuff! Grrrrrrrrr! Wuff, wuff, wuff, wuff! GRRRRRRRRRRRRRRRR!'

There had been a growl mixed up with the bark, and so Buttercup growled as well as barked. The other cows, who all disliked and feared dogs, were terrified almost out of their lives. They rushed off to the other end of the field in a fright.

As for Buttercup, she was terribly frightened

too! She hated dogs, and this bark and growl she had made her very much afraid. She galloped away – and trod so heavily on Pinkity's toe that he yelled with pain. He limped off crying big tears down his cheeky little face, and went home to bathe his poor foot.

So when Buttercup went to find him to beg him to take her bark away, he was nowhere to be seen! No – he was safely at home, tying up his poor squashed toe in a bandage, wishing very much that he hadn't played such silly tricks on foolish Buttercup!

Buttercup barked all through the night, and growled when she wasn't barking. Her friends were so frightened of her that they wouldn't let her come near them.

'If you come any nearer we will run our horns into you!' they cried. 'You are turning into a dog, there's no doubt! You will have to live in a kennel and eat biscuits and bones, instead of sweet grass.'

Buttercup was very unhappy. She went away into a corner and barked all to herself. 'Why did I bother about my voice?' she thought sadly. 'I would rather have no moo at all than bark like a dog. This is dreadful. What will the farmer say when he milks me?'

The farmer was scared and puzzled when he heard Buttercup's new voice. He stared at her as if he couldn't believe his ears. A cow barking? What next?

'Wuff, wuff!' said Buttercup, hanging her head in shame. 'Wuff, grrrrr!'

'I shall have to sell you, Buttercup,' said the farmer, seeing how frightened of her all the other cows seemed to be. 'I can't have a barking cow.'

'Wuff, grrr!' said Buttercup, most unhappily. She couldn't bear the thought of being sold. It would be dreadful to leave the fields she knew and go somewhere strange.

All that day she barked and growled, and

when night came she looked out anxiously for Pinkity. That rascally little creature had been feeling sorry that he had played such tricks on Buttercup. His toe was very painful, and he thought it must be a punishment for him.

'I'd better go out and see how Buttercup is tonight,' he thought to himself. 'Even though I can hardly walk, I must certainly go.'

So out he went into the field. No sooner had he gone through the gate than he almost jumped out of his skin. He heard what seemed to him to be a very fierce dog barking and growling just above him. Of course, it was Buttercup waiting for him. What a fright he got!

'Wuff, wuff, grrrrr!' said Buttercup. 'Do pray take this terrible voice away, Pinkity. Wuff! I frighten everyone and myself too. I would rather have no voice at all. It was foolish of me to want one.'

Pinkity took the bark and growl away and wrapped them carefully in his handkerchief. Then he limped off to find Bobby, who, he was sure, would be wanting his bark badly.

So he was. He was very angry indeed about it!

'You said you only wanted my bark for a little while!' he scolded. 'Here I've had to be all day without either my bark or my growl and couldn't even bark at an old tramp who came and stole some eggs. Give me my bark at once!'

49

Pinkity gave it to him – and then forgot all about his bad foot, for angry old Bobby chased him up the lane and over the fields, barking at the top of his voice!

'Wuff! You mischievous creature! Grrrrr! You scamp, you rogue! Wuff, grrr, wuff!'

Buttercup was very thankful indeed to have lost her bark. She ate the grass quietly, and when her friends saw that she no longer barked or growled they came round her once again and talked to her.

And suddenly she found herself mooing to them! Yes – her cold had gone away, and she had got her own voice back once more! It had gone only for a little while whilst she had a cold. So she needn't have worried herself so much after all!

'To think I had a quack, a squeak, a baa, a bark and a growl!' said Buttercup to herself, in shame. 'When all the time, if only I'd been patient, my own voice was just waiting to come back. Really, I am a very foolish cow! I do hope the farmer won't sell me now.'

He didn't, of course. When he found that Buttercup was her own self again, and mooed just as she always did, he patted her and said: 'Well, well – I can't think what happened to you yesterday, Buttercup – but you seem all right today, so, as you give me a nice lot of creamy milk, I shan't sell you!'

'Moo, moo, moo!' said Buttercup, and whisked her tail happily. Then she whisked it again and knocked off the farmer's hat. But he didn't seem to mind!

6

Lazy Luke

Once upon a time Lazy Luke fell asleep in front of his fire, and when he woke up it had gone out. He shivered.

'Look at that now – the fire's out and I've no more wood. I'll go and borrow a bundle from Dame Hurry-About.'

So he went across the road to Dame Hurry-About's cottage and asked her for some wood.

'You lazy fellow!' she said. 'Why don't you go to the woods and pick some up – there's plenty there!'

'It's a long way,' said Lazy Luke. 'You just lend me a few sticks, Dame Hurry-About, and I'll bring you plenty tomorrow.'

'Well, you do something for *me* first,' said Dame Hurry-About. 'You go and ask Mr Borrow-A-Lot to let me have back the teapot of mine I lent him yesterday. Then I'll let you have some sticks.'

'Oh bother! He lives up the hill,' said Lazy Luke.

'Well, no teapot, no sticks,' said Dame Hurry-About, so Luke had to go. He walked up the hill to Mr Borrow-A-Lot and saw him sitting down having a cup of tea out of Dame Hurry-About's teapot.

'Dame Hurry-About says, please will you give me her teapot that you borrowed yesterday,' said Lazy Luke.

'Well, as you can see, I'm using it,' said Mr Borrow-A-Lot. 'But I'll be finished in five minutes. You just pop down to Mother Cranky's and ask her if she can spare me a new-laid egg. She said she might have one for me today.'

'Oh *dear*!' said Lazy Luke. 'All that way! No, I'll sit down and wait till you're ready to give me the teapot.'

'Oh no you won't,' said Mr Borrow-A-Lot. 'No new-laid egg, no teapot!'

So Lazy Luke went off to Mother Cranky's, and he had to knock at her door four times before she opened it.

'Now, now, now, who's this waking me up out of my nap!' she said crossly. 'Oh, it's you, Lazy Luke. What do you want?'

'Mr Borrow-A-Lot says you promised him a new-laid egg today,' said Lazy Luke. 'I've come to get it for him.'

'Well, fancy you putting yourself out to do a job for anyone!' said Mother Cranky. 'That

53

does surprise me! I'll have to go and look in my hen-house to see if there's an egg there. You do something for me while I'm looking. Pop over to Father Hoo-Ha's and ask him to let you have his ladder for me. I just want to borrow it till tomorrow, to clean the top shelves of my larder.'

'But I don't want to have to carry a ladder all the way back here!' said Lazy Luke in horror!

'All right. No ladder, no new-laid egg,' said Mother Cranky, and shut the door in his face.

'I'll fetch the ladder, I'll fetch it!' shouted Lazy Luke. 'You get the egg!' And away he went again, grumbling loudly.

'Fetching and carrying like this! What do people think I am? An errand-boy?'

He came to Father Hoo-Ha's little house and knocked at the door. But Father Hoo-Ha wasn't indoors, he was right at the bottom of his garden. So Lazy Luke had to go round the back way and walk all the way down to him.

'And what's brought *you* so far from your fireside today?' said Father Hoo-Ha.

'Mother Cranky says, please will you lend her your ladder?' asked Lazy Luke.

'What! Do you mean to say you've offered to carry it to her?' said Father Hoo-Ha, astonished. 'Wonders will never cease. Well, it's in my shed, so I'll have to get it out. You go round to Mr Long-Whiskers while I'm getting it, and ask him to lend me his bicycle, please. He always lends it to me when I want it.'

'Oh *no*,' said Lazy Luke. 'No, I can't do that! I can't ride a bicycle and I'm not going to walk all the way back here pushing one!'

'Well, then – no ladder,' said Father Hoo-Ha, turning back to his gardening. 'No bicycle, no ladder – see?'

Lazy Luke did see. He sighed. 'I'll get the bicycle – but all I hope is that Mr Long-Whiskers hasn't got a job *he* wants doing as well. I'm tired of doing jobs.'

'Tired? You're always tired, you are, Lazy Luke!' said Father Hoo-Ha. 'It's a wonder to me you ever get up in the morning, it really is. Well now, do go along, or I shall have the ladder ready for you before you're back!'

Lazy Luke went off, groaning. His legs felt shaky and his head ached. Oh how tired he felt, doing so many things for so many people!

Mr Long-Whiskers was baking cakes, and he wasn't very pleased to see Lazy Luke. 'What do you want?' he said. 'You're just in time to do a job for me. Look, my oven isn't hot enough. Will you just pop out to the wood behind my house and bring back some wood for it?'

'No, I won't,' said Lazy Luke. 'Good gracious, that's what *I* wanted for my own fire, and here I've come for miles and done all kinds of jobs so that I can borrow some from Dame Hurry-About! If I'd wanted to fetch wood I'd have done it for myself, not for you!'

Mr Long-Whiskers picked up a broom and gave Lazy Luke a hard spank with it. 'You do as you're told!' he said. 'You haven't told me yet why you've come.'

'Oh – to borrow your bicycle for Father Hoo-Ha,' said Lazy Luke. 'Please don't spank me again with that broom. I'll go and get the wood for you!'

And away he hurried to the wood, gathered a great armful of dead wood, and hurried back. He did hope that Mr Long-Whiskers had put that broom away!

He had – and he had got the bicycle out ready for Lazy Luke. 'Oh, thanks,' said Lazy Luke and wheeled it off at once. But he was so tired that he really felt as if he must ride it. So he tried – and fell off at once. Goodness, what a crash! He bumped his head very badly indeed, and after that he decided to wheel the bicycle. He came to Father Hoo-Ha's and asked him for the ladder.

'Here's the bicycle,' he said. 'Oh my goodness – what an enormous ladder! Haven't you a smaller one?'

'No,' said Father Hoo-Ha. 'Ha – perhaps it will do your lazy bones good, carrying that all the way to Mother Cranky!'

56

Poor Lazy Luke. He staggered along to Mother Cranky's with the enormous ladder, and let it drop in her garden with a sigh of relief. He knocked at the kitchen door.

'I've brought the ladder,' he said. 'Can I have the egg?'

'Egg? What egg?' said Mother Cranky. 'Bless us all, what do you mean?'

'You said you'd give me a new-laid egg for Mr Borrow-A-Lot if I fetched that ladder,' said Lazy Luke. 'You did, you did!'

'Dear me, yes – I remember,' said Mother

Cranky. 'You've been so long that I'd forgotten about it. Here it is.' Lazy Luke took it and went off to Mr Borrow-A-Lot. Goodness, how far he had walked! He looked at his shoes – just see, one of his toes was poking through his shoe! Now he would have to pay for it to be mended!

He came to Mr Borrow-A-Lot's house and looked in at the window. Well, he was still having cups of tea out of Dame Hurry-About's teapot! Would you believe it! Lazy Luke was so cross that he walked straight in at the door without knocking.

'Manners, manners!' said Mr Borrow-A-Lot. 'You want the teapot, I suppose? You've been so long that I've brewed another pot. Have a cup?'

'*No*,' said Lazy Luke angrily, and put the new-laid egg down on the table. 'You ought to have had it washed and ready for me.'

'You can go and wash it yourself if you talk like that,' said Mr Borrow-A-Lot. 'And by the way – could you lend me ten pence? I don't seem to have any money left.'

'Ho! Haven't you! How strange – neither have I, Mr Borrow-A-Lot!' said Lazy Luke. He took the teapot and rinsed it angrily under the tap. Really, the things he had done this afternoon! He would have made a fortune if everyone had paid him for his work! He took

58

the teapot to Dame Hurry-About's, and, oh dear, what was this? There was a note on the door for Lazy Luke. This is what it said: 'To Lazy Luke. I got tired of waiting for you. Leave my teapot on the doorstep. You can come for the wood tomorrow morning at ten o'clock. Dame Hurry-About.'

'Well! WELL! So all those jobs had been done for nothing – he couldn't wait till tomorrow to have wood for his fire. He would freeze to death in his little cottage. Lazy Luke put the teapot down and began to sniffle.

'Why didn't I get my own wood? Now I've got to go and find some, and I'm so tired and cold. I've walked so far. I've fallen off a bicycle and bumped my head. I've done lots of silly jobs. All because I was too lazy to fetch my own wood! Oooh-hoo-hoo!' And off he went to the woods, crying tears down the front of his suit. Poor Lazy Luke. We could give you some good advice – but what's the use? You'd never take it!

7

The magic rubber

Once upon a time Snooty the gnome found a most remarkable rubber. It lay on the ground, in the middle of the woodland path, a large, long rubber, pointed at one end, and round at the other.

'What a curious thing!' said Snooty, picking it up. 'It must be magic. I wonder what it does.'

He rubbed it idly against a young birch tree – and to his immense surprise the tree vanished!

'I've rubbed it out!' said Snooty, in amazement. 'Oooh! What a very magic rubber this is! It rubs things out!'

He went to a blackberry bush and rubbed the leaves with the rubber. They disappeared at once. Then Snooty rubbed a few toadstools with the strange rubber. They vanished too! How very astonishing!

'Hoo!' said Snooty, in delight. 'This rubber will be very useful to me. I can think of a whole lot of things I'd like to rub out!'

Snooty put the rubber carefully into his

pocket. Then he danced home, singing and whistling, for he was very pleased to think he had found such a wonderful thing.

He didn't tell anyone about the magic rubber. He meant to have a good time with it without anyone knowing! The first thing he did when he got home was to get out his best pair of shoes and rub a nail that was sticking up into the heel part. It always tore his sock – but now he could get rid of it!

Sure enough, the nail disappeared at once! The magic rubber rubbed it out! Snooty was pleased. He looked round to see what else he could rub out.

'Oh, yes,' said Snooty, 'I'll rub out the door between the kitchen and the hall. It's always swinging and banging, and I don't need it!'

So he rubbed the door out with his rubber! It was marvellous to see it go! It just went.

Then Snooty saw in his garden Whiskers, the black cat from old Dame Topknot next door. Now Snooty hated this cat because it sat on his flower-beds, and spat at him if he went near it. So he looked at it with a grin, and said, 'Ha! I'll rub you out, Whiskers!'

And out he went with the magic rubber – and do you know, he rubbed that black cat out! One minute Whiskers was there, and the next he wasn't! It was most extraordinary!

Snooty was delighted. What a fine rubber he

had found! He looked over the high wall and saw that Dame Topknot had a plum-tree full of ripe plums. If only he could get some! He knew Dame Topknot was out, for he had seen her go by with her shopping-basket.

'I can't climb this high wall – but I can rub it out!' he said. 'Good! I'll rub a neat hole in it, get through it, and take some of those plums before Dame Topknot gets back!'

So he rubbed part of the wall with the large rubber – and he rubbed so many bricks out that a big hole came. Snooty climbed through it and filled his pockets with plums! What a feast he would have!

Snooty had a good time with his magic rubber! He rubbed out a dog that came into his front garden. He rubbed out all the wasps that came sailing into his kitchen. He rubbed out a mess he made when he spilt a pail of dirty water over the floor! Dear me, the things he rubbed out!

And then Snooty did a very silly thing! The next day he heard a rat-tat at his door and he went to open it. Outside was Mister Biscuit the baker, with his bill. Snooty hadn't paid Mister Biscuit for a very long time, and he owed him a lot of money. Mister Biscuit had come to ask for it. He walked into Snooty's kitchen and put his bill on the table.

'Will you please pay me for the bread and

the cakes and the pies you have had?' he asked.

'I haven't any money at present,' said Snooty. 'I will pay you next week.'

'That is what you always say!' said Mister Biscuit angrily. 'I won't listen to you any longer!' And he banged his fist so hard on the wooden table that a teapot jumped off and fell to the ground – crash!

'You careless fellow, look what you've done!' shouted Snooty, in a rage.

'Pay me my bill and I'll give you two pounds to buy a new teapot!' said Mister Biscuit, his long beard bristling.

'Never!' said Snooty. 'Take yourself off, and take that dreadful beard with you!'

'It's a beautiful beard!' shouted Mister Biscuit.

'It ought to be cut off and made into a yard-broom for sweeping up rubbish!' cried Snooty rudely. And do you know what he did? He took out his rubber and rubbed out Mister Biscuit's beard! Mister Biscuit did look funny without it.

'What have you done?' he wept. 'Oh, my beautiful, beautiful beard! It took me forty years to grow it!'

'Well, grow it again,' said Snooty, 'and grow your hair again too!'

He rubbed Mister Biscuit's hair – and that

went as well! Mister Biscuit gave a squeal of fright and rushed out of Snooty's house. He ran down the street, weeping.

Everyone came out to see what was the matter, and when they heard how Snooty had rubbed out Mister Biscuit's beard and hair they were very angry.

'That is the magic rubber belonging to the Wizard Hurry-up,' they said. 'He will be very annoyed when he knows it has been used by Snooty. Let us go and tell him. No doubt that rubber has rubbed out Dame Topknot's cat, and made that hole in her wall, and rubbed out

Gobo's dog too. Dear, dear, to think that Snooty might rub us all out if he wanted to!'

The Wizard Hurry-up was angry when he heard that Snooty had found and used his rubber. He strode off at once to Snooty's cottage and banged so hard at the door that Snooty nearly jumped up to the ceiling with fright.

Snooty was too much afraid to open the door, but the wizard didn't wait – he just flung the door open and walked in.

'Where's my rubber?' he shouted to Snooty.

Snooty took it out of his pocket and gave it to Hurry-up without a word. Hurry-up took it and then rubbed it in three places on the ceiling and in four places on the walls. Big holes appeared!

'Other people can play about with a magic rubber too!' said Hurry-up. 'But I don't expect you'll be pleased when the rain and the wind come through these holes, Snooty. Next time you find something belonging to somebody else just think twice before you take it and use it in such bad ways!'

He went away, and Snooty stared dolefully at the big holes in his roof and walls. The wind blew through, and he shivered. Oh, dear! It would take him such a long time to mend those holes!

Snooty worked hard for a whole week mending the seven big holes – and then he saw, in his back garden, Whiskers, Dame Topknot's cat, sitting down on his flower-bed again. He stared and stared – for he knew that he had rubbed Whiskers out with his magic rubber.

And then he saw Gobo's dog in his front garden – and then he saw his kitchen-door swinging and banging just as it used to before he rubbed it out!

Snooty ran to the Wizard Hurry-up and told him what had happened. 'Everything has come back again,' he said. 'Did you know it would, Hurry-up?'

'Oh, yes,' said Hurry-up grinning. 'The magic lasts only a week – then whatever was rubbed out comes back again!'

'And would the bits of my roof and ceiling that you rubbed out have come back again too?' asked Snooty.

'Of course,' said Hurry-up.

'And here I've been working hard all week long trying to mend those holes!' groaned Snooty. 'What a waste of time and money – and how my poor back aches!'

'It serves you right!' said Hurry-up.

'You are very horrid,' said Snooty.

'If you talk to me like that I'll get my rubber and rub *you* out!' said Hurry-up. 'Now let me see, where did I put it – in this drawer, I think!'

But before Hurry-up could get his rubber,

Snooty was gone. You couldn't see him for dust! He wasn't going to be rubbed out, not he!

Mister Biscuit's hair and beard came back again, and he went marching off to Snooty's with his bill once more. And Snooty paid it without a word. And how he has behaved himself since that week! He's always afraid Hurry-up will be after him to rub him out, you see!

8

The little blue kitten

'What's that sitting on Dame Grumpy's window-sill across the road?' said Gobbo, looking out of his front door.

'Good gracious! It looks like a kitten – but it can't be, because it's as blue as the sky!' said his brother Winky.

'Let's go and see,' said Gobbo. So they ran across and leaned over the wall. 'Yes,' said Gobbo, 'it *is* a blue kitten. Well, I've never in my life seen a blue kitten before. Puss, Puss, Puss!'

Dame Grumpy looked out of the window at once. 'Now, just you leave my kitten alone!' she said. 'I know you two mischievous little goblins! If you dare to tease my blue kitten I'll rub spells on your noses and make them grow as long as cucumbers!'

'Oh no, please don't,' said Gobbo, in alarm. 'We're not mischievous, really we're not. You're thinking of our cousins Hoppy and Jumpy – they really *are* naughty. We only just came to look at your blue kitten. I suppose you wouldn't let us play with it sometimes? We could give it an empty cotton-reel to roll about – it would love that.'

'You leave my blue kitten alone!' said Dame Grumpy. 'If I see you anywhere near it I'll come after you with my Spanking Slipper!'

'Meow!' said the kitten, looking at Gobbo and Winky.

'There! It's talking to us!' said Gobbo, very pleased. But Dame Grumpy picked it up and went indoors with it at once.

'We'd better be careful,' said Gobbo. 'I don't like that Spanking Slipper of hers. Let's go back.'

Well, the two little goblins didn't go near the blue kitten. They just waved to it when they went out to do their shopping, but that was all. Then one day as they took their big round basket with them to shop at the market, they saw that the kitten wasn't on Dame Grumpy's window-sill as usual.

'It must be indoors,' said Gobbo – and just at that minute Dame Grumpy came out, calling 'Puss, Puss, Puss!' Then she saw the two goblins and frowned.

'Have you taken my kitten to play with? You know what I told you – I'll rub a spell on your noses and . . .'

'Please, Dame Grumpy, we haven't seen the

69

kitten this morning,' said Gobbo, in a hurry, backing away quickly. 'We've never even stroked it, though we'd like to!'

'Well, if I see you with it, I'll spank you, just as I said,' said Dame Grumpy. 'Puss, Puss, Puss, where have you gone to? Oh dear – I do hope it hasn't run away!'

'Come on, let's go and do our shopping,' said Gobbo. 'My goodness – I'd certainly run away from Dame Grumpy if I was her kitten – wouldn't you, Winky?'

They went off down the road. They were soon at the market, and bought such a lot of things: six rosy apples; six big brown eggs; some butter; a round chocolate cake; and a string of nice fat sausages. The basket was quite full by the time they had finished. They set off home again – and then, just as they passed under a big chestnut tree, they heard a sound that made them both stop at once.

'Meow! Meeee-ow! Meeeeeee-ow!'

'That's a cat mewing – and it's frightened!' said Winky at once. 'Where is it? Puss, Puss, Puss!'

'Mee-ow-ee-ow-ee-ow!' said the cat, wher-ever it was.

'It sounds as if it's up this big tree,' said Gobbo, and he looked up into the branches. 'Yes – it is! And, Winky – it's the little blue kitten!'

70

'So it is!' said Winky, peering up too. 'It must have wandered away from Dame Grumpy's and climbed up this tree. Perhaps a dog frightened it.'

'Come down, kitty!' called Gobbo. 'Come along. We'll take care of you. You needn't be frightened of dogs.'

'Meeeee-ow-ow!' said the kitten, sadly, and didn't move at all. It was much too frightened. The ground looked a long way away, and it was afraid of falling. It had never been up a tree before, and it didn't much like it now it was there.

'Little kittens shouldn't climb big trees,' said Gobbo, looking up at it. 'Winky, what can we do? We can't leave it there. It might never come down.'

'Well, I'll climb up and see if I can get it,' said Gobbo, and up he went. But as soon as he came near the kitten it climbed a little higher! But at last Gobbo managed to catch it and it snuggled into his arms.

'Oh good!' called Winky. 'Come on down.'

'I can't!' said Gobbo. 'I want my arms to climb down with, but I can't use them because I'm holding the kitten. I shall fall if I don't use my arms. Oh dear, don't wriggle so, kitten. Winky, what shall we do?'

'I don't know,' said Winky, and he frowned. Then a good idea came into his head. 'Gobbo!'

71

he called, 'shall I empty out all the things in our basket, and climb up the tree with it? We could put the kitten into it, and lower it down the tree.'

'But what shall we lower it with?' said Gobbo.

'I'll pop into Ding-Dong's house, and ask him if he'll lend me his kite-string,' said Winky. So he ran to Ding-Dong's house, and Ding-Dong said yes, certainly he could borrow his kite-string. So it wasn't long before Winky was back again. He emptied everything out of the basket, and tied the string to the handle. Then he climbed up the tree with the basket.

'Here we are!' he said to Gobbo. 'Now – put the kitten very carefully in the basket. I'll climb down, and you can let the basket swing down to the ground. I'll be there to take out the kitten.' Well, they were *just* doing that when Gobbo gave a yell that almost made Winky fall out of the tree.

'Winky, quick! Look, there's that wicked little Hoppy down there – and Jumpy too – and they're picking up all our shopping. Quick, climb down and stop them!' Winky climbed down so fast that he almost lost his footing! But when he came to the bottom of the tree, Hoppy and Jumpy had gone – and so had the brown eggs, the rosy apples, the butter, the nice fat sausages and the

round chocolate cake! Oh, those bad little
goblins!

'Just wait till I see them!' said Winky, almost
in tears. 'Gobbo, swing the basket down now,
gently, very gently. Oooh – careful! I do hope
the kitten won't jump out!'

The kitten lay quietly as the basket swung
down – and even when Winky caught it, the
little thing didn't move. It seemed to like the
basket, it gave a little purr, shut its eyes and
went to sleep!

'Dear little kitten!' said Winky. 'Oh dear – I'm glad to have rescued you, but you've made us lose all our shopping!'

Gobbo climbed down and the two goblins went off, carrying the sleeping kitten in the basket – and whom should they meet round the corner, but Dame Grumpy!

'Oh my goodness!' said Gobbo, and stopped. But it was too late – Dame Grumpy had seen the kitten in their basket.

'*You* had my kitten after all!' she cried. 'You took it away in your basket! I'll put a spell on your noses to make them long as cucumbers! I'll get my Spanking Slipper, I'll . . .' But the goblins didn't wait to hear any more. They fled down the road, and into their house with the kitten – and slammed and locked the door! When Dame Grumpy came panting up, they called from their bedroom window.

'You shan't have your kitten back till you promise not to put a spell on us. It was up a tree and we rescued it! We emptied our shopping-basket and borrowed Ding-Dong's kite-string, and let it down in the empty basket – and while we were doing that Hoppy and Jumpy stole all our shopping.'

'You get us back our shopping and you can have your kitten!' shouted Winky.

'Is this all true?' said Dame Grumpy. 'Well, I'm very, very sorry I chased you. I'll make a spell straight away to bring back your shopping!' And hey presto, she waved her stick in the air and muttered some strange magic words.

Good gracious! What was this flying through the air? A string of sausages! Six brown eggs, followed by six rosy apples! A pat of butter and a round chocolate cake! They all came quietly to rest on the garden seat. Gobbo and Winky could hardly believe their eyes.

'Now come on down with my blue kitten,' said Dame Grumpy. 'You're very kind. I'm sorry I was so cross – but it isn't often that goblins are helpful, you know.'

So Gobbo and Winky came down into the garden, carrying the sleeping kitten in the basket. It looked so sweet and comfortable. 'We'll lend you the basket till it wakes up,' said Winky. 'Please – do you think we could come and play with it sometimes?'

'Of course. Whenever you like!' said Dame Grumpy. 'But just let me warn you – keep indoors for the next ten minutes. I'm sending my Spanking Slipper after those two bad goblins, Happy and Jumpy!'

So Gobbo and Winky kept safely indoors – and goodness me, they saw that Spanking Slipper hopping along the road, looking for the goblins!

'There it goes, looking for Hoppy and Jumpy,' said Gobbo, with a giggle. 'My word – won't they get a shock when it hops into their kitchen!'

They will – but I don't feel a bit sorry for them, do you?

9

Oh, Flibberty-Gibberty!

Now once, on a lovely windy spring morning, little Flibberty-Gibberty felt full of glee. He leapt and he danced as he went through the primrose woods, and he shouted for joy. Then, just for fun, he pretended that something was after him. 'I must run, I must run!' he shouted at the top of his voice. 'The Big Blustery Breeze is after me! Ooooh!'

He leapt into the air as he ran, like a little mad thing. 'Ooooh! It's after me! The Big Blowing Blustery Breeze is after me! It'll blow me to the moon! It'll sweep me to the stars! Make way, make way. I'm running for my life. Ooooh!'

The rabbits leapt out of his way in fright. A robin trilled after him, 'Tirra-tatta, what's the matter?' But little Flibberty-Gibberty wouldn't stop.

A squirrel ran up a tree out of his way, and Flibberty-Gibberty raced by, his cloak blowing out like a sail. 'Ooooh! Get out of my way! I shall be caught by the Big Blowing Blustery Breeze.'

A little fawn jumped out of his way just in time, and stared after him with big startled eyes.

Why was Flibberty-Gibberty acting like this? Who was after him? The little fawn was frightened and raced after the pixie at top speed.

Then some rabbits ran after the fawn, afraid too. What was this Big Blowing Blustery Thing that Flibberty was shouting and leaping and dancing about?

The brownies smiled to see the mad little pixie go leaping. Whatever would he do next? One called after him.

'Flibberty-Gibberty, be careful of the Wandering Wizard. He's about this morning, and he's in a very bad temper. Don't you let him turn you into a toadstool and sit on you, as he did to Bron the Brownie!'

That made Flibberty-Gibberty slow down a little. The Wandering Wizard – oooh! He wasn't very nice. Nobody liked him much, but nobody could catch him, because he was much too clever.

But then Flibberty forgot about the wizard, and went flying through the woods as lightly as an autumn leaf, leaping and bounding as he went, still pretending to be scared to death!

And then, round a tree, who should he bump into and knock right over but the Wandering Wizard himself! My goodness me, what a thing to do! The Wizard went over like a wooden skittle and lay there, all his breath knocked out of him.

'Out of my way!' shouted Flibberty-Gibberty, not seeing who it was at first. 'The Big Blowing Blustery Breeze is after me – oooh!'

'What's that?' cried the Wandering Wizard, clutching Flibberty by the ankle. '*Who's* coming? What's happening? My goodness, look at this fawn coming at top speed – and all these rabbits. *What's happening, I say!*'

'Let go my ankle! Run, run!' shouted the little pixie. 'Run! I tell you the Big Blustering Blowing Breeze is coming! It'll blow you to the moon! It'll sweep you to the stars. Run!'

Just then the wind did blow, and very roughly too, so that the little clouds scudded across the sky like white rabbits. The Wizard felt quite scared. He still held Flibberty's ankle and wouldn't let go.

'Help me up!' he said. 'I don't know what to do. I'm too old to run away. Oh, this wind – *I* don't want to be blown to the moon! Flibberty-Gibberty, help me up, I say!'

'Well, let go my ankle then,' said Flibberty, quite fiercely. 'I must run. I tell you, the Big,

Blowing, Blustery Breeze is after me! Let me go!'

'You must help me first, before I let you go,' said the Wizard, and stood up very carefully. He held Flibberty's arm now, and still wouldn't let him go.

'Whooooooooosh!' said the wind, entering into the fun. It blew the Wizard's hat off, and Flibberty picked it up for him. The little pixie was frightened. Oh dear – he didn't want to be

taken away by this Wandering Wizard! *What* a
pity he had bumped into him.

'Whoooooooooosh!' said the wind again, and
tried to pull off the Wizard's flapping cloak.

'Take your fingers off me, you Blustery
Breeze!' shouted the Wizard in fright.
'Flibberty, what can I do? I'll be blown right
away, for my big cloak will act like a sail!'

'Climb up into a tree!' shouted Flibberty,
longing to get rid of the Wizard. 'I'll help you.'

So he helped him up into a tree – and then
the wind rushed down again in delight and
shook the tree so that it bent from side to side
and swayed like a ship!

'I shall be blown out!' shouted the Wizard.
'And here comes the wind again! Flibberty, I
shall be *blown out*, I tell you. Think of something!'

'Give me your girdle and I'll tie you safely to
the tree!' cried the pixie. 'Ooooh – your hat
might get blown to the moon. It will be waiting
there for you, when *you* arrive if I don't tie you
up. Give me your girdle!'

So the Wizard undid his girdle with one
hand, clinging to the swaying tree with the
other – and Flibberty tied him very, very tightly
to the tree. Oh, very tightly indeed!

'You needn't be afraid of the Big, Blowing
Blustery Breeze now!' shouted the pixie. 'If it
blows all day and all night you'll be safe here,

Wizard. Whooosh, here comes the wind again. Goodbye, goodbye – it's blowing me away again!'

And off he went once more, leaping, bounding just like the little fawn behind him, pretending to be dreadfully frightened. 'Oooh! I shall be caught. Make way for me, I shall be caught!'

But he wasn't caught. Nor was the little fawn, nor were the skippitty rabbits or the scampering squirrel. Only one person was caught and that was the Wandering Wizard tied so tightly to the tree. How he howled for help, as loudly as the wind! How he shook with rage, so that the tree swayed even more!

'Flibberty, come back! Untie me! Get me down! Flibberty, I'll turn you into a candle-flame and blow you out! I'll turn you into a lump of ice and melt you. I'll – I'll . . .'

But Flibberty-Gibberty was far away, tired out with all his leaping and jumping and pretending, fast asleep with the tired rabbits and squirrel and little fawn cuddled up to him. What a day! What a wonderful, blustery, windy day!

'It was fun,' said Flibberty in his dreams. 'Oh, it was FUN!'

10

Tippitty and the dolls' house

'What shall I do today?' said Ellen. 'I'm tired of all my toys, and I've read all my books!'

'Well then – what about giving your dolls' house a spring-clean?' said Mummy. 'I had a look at it yesterday and really it is too dirty and untidy for words!'

'Oh yes – I could do that!' said Ellen. 'Can I have a saucer of water, and a little cloth, Mummy?'

'Yes – and you can have this tiny little nail-brush to brush the carpets and scrub the floors,' said Mummy. 'It's such a nice dolls' house, and I'm sure the little dolls who live in it must feel very uncomfortable – everything is in such a muddle!'

Well, Ellen soon had a saucer of warm water with some soap powder in it. She had two little cloths, one for the windows and one for floors. Mummy gave her a tiny duster too, to polish the furniture.

It was certainly a pretty dolls' house from the

outside. It had white walls, a red roof, four chimneys, windows that opened – and a tiny garage at the side.

The whole front opened when Ellen wanted to play with the dolls' house. Even the lights switched on and off, and water came out of the taps from a small tank in the roof. Ellen could even fill the bath when she liked!

She began to spring-clean the house. She took down the curtains first. Then she took out the carpets and rugs. Then out came all the furniture, and soon the house was empty.

And then Ellen noticed a strange thing. The little dolls' house dolls weren't there!

'Where are they?' wondered Ellen. 'There should be four of them, all tiny little things. I haven't seen them for a long time – but then I haven't played with my dolls' house for ages.'

The toys who sat around watching Ellen could have told her what had happened to the tiny dolls! The teddy bear had been a great friend of theirs, and they had told him how they hated living in such a dirty, untidy little house.

'We'd clean it ourselves,' they said, 'but we haven't any cloths or brooms or dusters. We can hardly see out of the windows, they are so dirty!'

'Well, there's a lovely dolls' house in the toy-shop just down the road,' the teddy bear told them. 'There aren't any dolls in that. Why don't you slip out one night, and let me take you to the shop? Then you could live in that nice new dolls' house, and be sold with it, when somebody buys it!'

'That's a good idea,' said the oldest doll, a pretty little thing in a blue silk frock. 'We'll go tonight.'

And so that night the bear had opened the front door of the dolls' house and called in softly. 'Are you awake? I'm ready to take you!'

The dolls were awake. They all trooped out of the front door, and the oldest doll shut it quietly. 'I'm not a bit sorry to leave!' she said. 'Ellen never even comes near us, and hasn't played with us for weeks! Lead the way, Teddy, to our new home.'

And off they all went, out of the door, down the stairs, and through the kitchen door, which had been left open for the cat to come in. They soon arrived at the toy-shop, and the teddy bear lifted each tiny doll up to the letter-box on the front door, and slid her through it. It was lucky that the letter-box was so low down!

'Thank you!' the dolls called softly. 'We can see the lovely dolls' house. It will be fine to live in a clean house. Perhaps a nice little girl will buy it one day and we'll all go and live with *her*!'

So that was why Ellen's dolls' house had no

dolls living in it now! She simply couldn't *imagine* where they had gone to! She hunted for them everywhere, and the toys watched her, nudging one another.

'Wish we could tell her!' said the teddy bear. 'She would feel sorry she hadn't kept the dolls' house nice and clean then!'

'Sh!' said the big doll. 'She'll hear you! Now look – she's beginning to scrub the floors – about time too!'

It took Ellen the whole day to clean the dolls' house. She washed the curtains and Mummy ironed them. She cleaned the floors and the windows. She rubbed down the walls. She brushed each little carpet and each rug, and washed three that were very dirty indeed. Then she polished all the furniture – the little tables and chairs and cupboards, and the wardrobe that stood in the bedroom. She even polished the tiny bathroom taps, and put a very small towel on the rail there.

She filled the little tank in the roof with water, so that the taps would run properly.

'Now the bath can be filled too,' she said. 'But there isn't anyone to have a bath in it! Oh dear – *where* can my dolls have gone!'

Mummy was very pleased when she saw the spotless little house. 'Now your dolls will really *like* that,' she said. 'Where are they?'

'I don't know,' said Ellen. 'They've

disappeared. Do *you* know where they are, Mummy?'

'No, I don't,' said Mummy. 'They'll be here somewhere, I expect. I'll have a look round.'

But neither she nor Ellen could find the dolls. 'You'll have to save up and buy one or two,' said Mummy. 'It's a pity that that dear little house shouldn't have anyone living in it!'

The toys thought so too. The big doll went to look through the windows, and said how lovely it looked inside. The bear peeped in too, and wished he was small enough to sleep in one of the little beds. 'They look so cosy,' he said. 'I do wish we knew someone who would like this little house.'

Then the teddy bear remembered the pixie who lived in a hole in the apple tree, just outside the playroom window. He turned to the big doll in excitement.

'What about Tippitty the pixie?' he said. 'She's always saying how cold she is at night, even though she has stuffed the hole in the tree with dead leaves. Do you think *she* would like to live in the dolls' house now that it is so lovely and clean? She's just the right size!'

'Oh *yes*!' said the bear, who liked Tippitty very much. 'We'll ask her this very night.'

So they tapped seven times on the window-pane, which was a signal for Tippitty to come and see them. She flew in at the top of the window, and landed just beside them.

'What do you want?' she said. 'Oooh – I had to get out of my leafy bed – and it's *such* a cold night!'

'Come and see the dolls' house,' said the bear. 'It's clean and lovely now!'

Tippitty pressed her nose to one of the dolls' house windows and looked inside. The moon was shining brightly, and she could see everything clearly. It certainly did look very pretty and very cosy. 'I'd like to go in at the front door,' she said. 'Oh, what a pity – whoever cleaned the house forgot to clean the little brass knocker!'

She went in at the front door and explored the whole house, while the big toys watched her through the windows. She could hardly believe it when water came out of a tap she turned on – and she loved the little mirror on the dressing table. 'I've never had a mirror in my life!' she said. 'Oh – I *do* wish I could live here!'

'Well, you can,' said the big doll at once. 'The dolls who once lived here have run away to the toy-shop, so the house is empty. You come, Tippitty. We'd love you to!'

'But – suppose Ellen peeps inside!' said Tippitty. 'She might see me and catch me. I couldn't bear that!'

'You could easily hide in the big wardrobe in the bedroom,' said the bear. 'Oh do come, Tippitty. It would be fun to have you to play with each night. I'll keep the tank filled, so that you can have a bath whenever you want to. And when Ellen is out we could light a fire in the kitchen for you!'

'All right. I'd love to come,' said Tippitty. 'This very night! Shall I be able to sleep in this dear little bed – and wash myself in that little basin? I shall keep this house very, very clean and tidy if I live here!'

Well, she did go to live there and she is there still! She sleeps in the little bed, she has a bath when she wants to, and, when Ellen is out, the bear lights the little kitchen fire, and Tippitty sometimes bakes tiny fruit cakes for him!

And HOW tidy and clean she keeps the house! Ellen's mother is always so pleased when she looks in at the window to see it.

'Well, really, Ellen keeps her dolls' house beautifully now!' she says. 'What a pity no one lives in it. I do wonder where those little dolls went to!'

Ellen herself is very puzzled. One morning she looked in at the bedroom window of the dolls' house and saw that the little bed wasn't made!

And then she noticed that the tiny brass knocker on the front door was bright and shining!

'Good gracious! Surely nobody is *living* here!' she thought. 'Is one of my dolls back – or is it a small mouse who likes a cosy bed? I must look into every little room and see.'

So she looked in the kitchen and the sitting-room and the bathroom and the bedroom, and even the garage. But she didn't see anyone at all.

Tippitty was hiding in the wardrobe, of course, shivering with fright. Oh, dear – would Ellen find her there and turn her out?

But Ellen didn't once think of looking in the wardrobe. So Tippitty is still living in the dolls' house, but now she is careful to make her bed as soon as she jumps out of it.

You'll know where to look for her if ever you go to tea with Ellen! Inside the wardrobe!

11

The little green imp

The Prince of Ho-Ho had a very bad-tempered cook. None of the other servants liked her, but she was big and strong, and nobody dared to complain of her.

They had a very bad time until Twinkle, the kitchen-boy, came to work there. Mrs Pudding, the cook, made him get up at five o'clock in the morning, and would not let him go to bed until midnight, and the poor boy was working hard all the time.

But Twinkle had a grandmother who was half a witch, and when he got out one afternoon to run an errand he went to his grandmother's cottage in the wood.

'Granny!' he said, 'tell me what to do! There's a cook at the castle, and she gives me a dreadful time, and everyone else too! How can I stop her?'

His granny thought for a moment, and then she nodded her head. 'Wait a minute!' she said. 'I've just the thing for you!'

She took a big green dish and filled it full of water. She scattered a green powder into it and it changed the water to a brilliant emerald. She peeled a potato into it, stirred it round with a peacock's feather, and muttered words so magic that Twinkle felt a bit frightened.

'Watch!' said his granny. He looked into the bowl, and suddenly out of the green water there jumped a green imp with a potato body and a grinning face! He smacked his hands together and looked up at Twinkle's grandmother.

'You'll do!' said the old lady, and she laughed. 'Here, Twinkle, put him into your pocket. As soon as you get into the kitchen, put him on a shelf and leave him. He will do the rest!'

Twinkle thanked his grandmother and put the green imp into his pocket. The imp laughed out loud and pinched him once or twice, but Twinkle didn't mind. He guessed that the imp would play a few tricks on Mrs Pudding, the bad-tempered cook!

As soon as he got into the kitchen he put the imp on the shelf behind a saucepan. Mrs Pudding turned round and scolded Twinkle. 'What have you been so long for, you good-for-nothing boy?'

'Now, Cookie, you be good!' said the voice of the green imp suddenly from the shelf. 'Naughty, naughty, naughty!'

Mrs Pudding turned round in a rage, too astonished to speak. The green imp peeped at her from behind a saucepan and made a face.

'And what are *you* doing in my kitchen, I'd like to know!' said Mrs Pudding, her eyes gleaming with rage. 'Come here!'

But that little imp stayed where he was, rapping out a tune on one of the saucepans, and grinning with all his might. 'Oh, Cookie, what a naughty temper!' he shouted.

The other servants were all staring in delight and astonishment. How could that green imp dare to speak to Mrs Pudding like that? The cook went over to the shelf and put out her hand to get the imp, but he picked up a fork lying nearby and rapped her fingers hard. Then he pushed six saucepans on to the floor, one after another – bang! – crash! – smash! – bang! – crash! – smash! – what a dreadful noise they made! Mrs Pudding was very angry.

She picked up a newspaper and folded it so that she might hit the little imp with it. She brought it down on the shelf – bang! Two more saucepans and a kettle jumped off to the ground – bang! – crash! – clang! The imp was nowhere to be seen.

'That's finished *him*!' said Mrs Pudding, pleased. But, dear me, it hadn't! No, he had just jumped neatly off the shelf on to the kitchen table behind the cook. And on the

table he saw a jug of milk. The imp grinned. He picked it up by the handle, jumped up on to the mantelpiece, and tilted the jug over Mrs Pudding's head!

Trickle, trickle, trickle! The milk fell on her head and ran down her neck! She got such a shock! How that imp laughed! He nearly fell off the mantelpiece with laughing. As for Twinkle and the other servants, they roared too. But Mrs Pudding got angrier and angrier.

She picked up a large cabbage and flung it at the imp. He dodged it neatly and it hit the kitchen clock. Crash! Down came the clock and a big tea-caddy, and the cabbage too! The cook stared in horror!

'Oh, naughty, naughty, naughty!' said the imp, dancing about on the table again, where he had jumped.

Mrs Pudding turned round to him, and the wicked little thing threw an egg at her. It broke and went down her neck to join the milk. Oh dear – poor Mrs Pudding! What a sight she looked! The imp began to laugh so much that he was afraid he might be caught, so he jumped up on to another shelf and hid in a bucket there. Mrs Pudding looked all round for him, and when she could not find him she went to wash the egg off herself.

'How dare you all stand grinning there?' she cried to the other servants. 'Get on with your work at once, and if you see that green imp anywhere about just catch him and bring him to me!'

But nobody meant to catch him. It was fun to see someone who was not afraid of Mrs Pudding! She washed herself and then boxed Twinkle's ears for upsetting some salt.

'Oh, naughty Cookie, oh, naughty Cookie!' squealed the voice of the green imp, and he popped his head out of the bucket. Mrs Pudding saw him.

'Oh, so you've turned up again, have you?'

she said. 'Well, I'll get you this time!' And with that she took the bucket down from the shelf, but the imp hopped out and ran into the larder crying, 'Can't catch *me*, can't catch *me*!'

Mrs Pudding rushed after him, but he was waiting for her. He threw a string of sausages round her neck and dropped a pat of butter neatly on her head from the top shelf. Really, you never knew what that wicked imp was going to do next!

All the evening things went on like that, and there was no catching that imp, and no stopping him either. Twice he emptied water over Mrs Pudding, and once he pelted her with apples he had found in a basket. Mrs Pudding rushed round and round the kitchen after him, but she couldn't seem to get hold of him at all. He was as slippery as an eel. He undid her shoe-laces when she wasn't looking. He undid her apron-strings and made her apron slip off a dozen times. He emptied pepper near her, and she sneezed thirty times without stopping.

'Oh, won't someone get rid of this horrid little imp for me!' wept Mrs Pudding at last. 'What has he come for?'

'I think he has come to tease you and torment you because you have treated *us* so badly,' said Twinkle boldly.

'That's right, that's right, that's right!' squealed the imp from somewhere under the table, where he was busy untying Mrs Pudding's shoe-laces again.

'If only you'd catch him and get rid of him for me I'd mend my ways and be better,' sobbed Mrs Pudding, who was quite tired out.

'Very well, then, I'll try,' said Twinkle, grinning to himself. He knew just what to do, for his granny had told him. He took a pat of butter, a dab of vinegar and a brown clove. He stuck the clove into the butter and smeared it with vinegar. Then he held it out to the imp.

The little green imp smelt the clove in the butter and came eagerly for it. Twinkle snatched him up and put him into his pocket.

'I'll go and give him to my old Granny,' he said to Mrs Pudding. 'She will know what to do with him, for she is half a witch.'

He ran off, chuckling to himself, and soon came to his grandmother's. When she heard his story, how she laughed! 'That will cure her bad temper!' she said. 'Tell Mrs Pudding that I will take the imp, but I shall not be able to keep him if she loses her temper again, for he will surely come back!'

So Twinkle left the green imp with his granny, who set him to work polishing her kettles and saucepans till they shone. He was afraid to do anything cheeky to the old dame. She had made him from a potato, and she could turn him back into one again!

As for Mrs Pudding, she didn't dare to lose her temper again, for she was so afraid the imp would turn up in her kitchen once more. So now everything is peace and quiet there, and Twinkle the kitchen-boy is as happy as can be.

But he can't help wishing Mrs Pudding would lose her temper once or twice – it *would* be such fun to see that imp dodging about the kitchen shouting, 'Naughty Cookie! Naughty, naughty!' at the top of his cheeky little voice. I'd rather like to see him myself, wouldn't you?

12

Winkle makes a mistake

Winkle was a mean and dishonest old gnome. If he found a bad coin he pretended it was a good one and gave it to a shopkeeper on a dark evening. If he could borrow anything and not return it, he did. His house was quite full of basins, brooms and plates he had borrowed and never taken back!

'You'll be sorry one day!' said the people who knew him. 'Yes you will! People like you don't get on well in this world!'

But Winkle only grinned – for he really got on very well indeed. He had a long red stocking put away full of money. He always had chicken every Saturday for dinner, which his black cat caught for him from the farm over the hill, and he always had warm clothes to wear in winter.

'I get on all right!' he said to himself. 'What's the sense of being honest if it keeps you poor? No, no – I'll go my own way and be rich!'

So he went on being mean and dishonest, and getting richer and richer.

Now one day he went shopping in the next town. He bought all kinds of things, and asked the shops to send them home to him. The only parcel he took home was a brown paper one with his mended shoes inside.

He caught the bus and sat down. Next to him was a very smart fellow, a gnome who lived in a big castle in the next village to Winkle. He took no notice of Winkle at all, although the gnome said 'Good morning.' He didn't like the look of Winkle, it was plain.

Winkle got out at his village, picked up the brown-paper parcel and walked home, feeling very cross with the fine gnome who hadn't said 'Good morning' to him. He put down his parcel and put on the kettle to boil.

After he had had a cup of cocoa and some bread and cheese he opened his parcel to take out his mended old shoes – and what a surprise he got!

In the parcel was a pair of very fine shoes indeed – oh, very fine ones, fit for a king to wear! They were of leather sewn with gold, and had gold laces threaded through, and buckles set with pearls. Winkle stared at them in astonishment.

'The old cobbler at the shop has put the wrong shoes in my parcel!' he thought to himself. 'Silly old fellow! How careless of him! Well, I'm not going to bother to give them back to him. He shouldn't have been so silly as to make that mistake! I shall keep them and wear them! Ho, ho!'

Wasn't he mean? He ought to have taken them back at once to the cobbler, of course. He put them away in his cupboard and longed for a party so that he might wear them and be very grand indeed.

Now it wasn't the cobbler who had made the mistake at all. He had put the right shoes in the gnome's parcel – Winkle's old mended ones. It was *Winkle* who had made a mistake – for in the bus he had sat next to the smart gnome who had also a parcel with him; and in *his* parcel was a pair of very fine shoes he had been to buy for His Majesty the King! Winkle hadn't looked to see that he was taking the right parcel when he jumped from the bus – he had picked up the parcel belonging to the other gnome and gone off with that.

So when the grand gnome arrived home and opened *his* parcel, what should he find but a pair of old mended shoes and he was most disgusted. He guessed at once what had happened. The other gnome in the bus, the one who had said 'Good morning' to him, must have taken the wrong parcel. Oh, well, it was annoying, but no doubt when the other fellow found out his mistake he would bring back the shoes.

But, of course, Winkle didn't. As you know, he put them into his cupboard and kept them for himself, thinking that the cobbler had made a mistake.

Now when the grand gnome didn't get the shoes brought back, and found that nobody had asked the bus-conductor about them, he decided to put up notices everywhere, to say what had happened, and to tell the gnome who had taken the wrong parcel where to bring the shoes. So he wrote some notices in red ink and stuck them up all over the place, in the villages round.

At the top of the notice he printed three words very large indeed. The words were: 'GOLD-LACED SHOES'. Anyone catching sight of those words and having the wrong shoes at home would be sure to read the notice, thought the grand gnome, and he would soon have the shoes back.

Well, it wasn't long before Winkle the gnome did see those notices, and read the words at the top: 'GOLD-LACED SHOES'. But he didn't read any further.

'It's only that silly old cobbler putting up notices about the shoes he gave me in mistake for my own,' thought Winkle. 'Well, if I don't read the notice, I can't find out anything more about the grand shoes, and as I don't *want* to find out anything, I shan't read the notice!'

So he didn't – and he was the only person in the village who didn't know that the shoes belonged to the King himself!

Well, when no one brought back the shoes to the grand gnome in his castle he became angry.

'Someone is keeping them for himself!' he thought. 'Oho! Well, I can soon stop that! Shoes, come to me, and clatter as you come!'

Then a most extraordinary thing happened. Those gold-laced shoes, put safely away in Winkle's cupboard, began to struggle to get out. They wriggled out of the door and began to make a clatter on the floor. Winkle heard them and ran to see what was the matter.

When he saw that the shoes were trying to get away he was surprised and angry and put them back into the cupboard again.

But once more they struggled out, almost breaking the door down! They wriggled away from Winkle's hands and danced downstairs. They shot out of the front door with Winkle after them and clattered off down the street, making a great noise.

'Stop! Come back!' yelled Winkle, who wasn't going to lose those fine shoes if he could help it. But the shoes took no notice at all. They just went on, making a great clatter all the way down the street. Then people poured out of their houses to see the strange sight, and followed Winkle and the shoes, laughing and

104

pointing. What an excitement for the village! Wherever were those shoes going?

The shoes went clattering to the next village and climbed up the steps of the castle where the grand gnome lived. He heard them coming and went to meet them. He saw behind them an angry gnome, trying in vain to catch hold of the dancing shoes.

'Take this man,' the big gnome ordered his servants. 'Bring him before me in my castle.'

He picked up the shoes, and strode inside, the servants following with the surprised Winkle between them. Winkle was truly amazed. Why was he suddenly treated like this?

He stood before the grand gnome.

'How came you to have these shoes?' asked the gnome sternly.

'Oh – the c-c-cobbler put them into my parcel by m-m-mistake,' stammered Winkle, in fright.

'Why didn't you take them back to him, then?' said the gnome.

'Well, if he was silly enough to make a mistake I thought he should be punished for it,' said Winkle, more boldly.

'I see,' said the gnome. 'You think if people make mistakes they deserve to be punished, even if they didn't mean to make them?'

'Certainly,' said Winkle.

'Well, listen to a little tale I have to tell of a gnome who made a big mistake,' said the grand gnome, in a stern voice. 'Once there were two gnomes in a bus, each with a brown-paper parcel. One gnome had old mended shoes in his parcel, but the other had gold-laced shoes he had bought for His Majesty the King. Now one of the gnomes got out of the bus first and by mistake took the wrong parcel.'

Winkle grew pale. How dreadful! So it wasn't the cobbler's mistake after all – it was *he*, Winkle, who had made a mistake!

'As you have just said,' went on the grand gnome, 'a mistake must be punished, even though it was not made on purpose! You will go to prison, or pay a fine of one thousand pounds to the poor people of the villages around! Oh, Winkle, you think I have not heard of you and your mean, dishonest ways – but your name is in everyone's mouth! You are rich – but only by wrong-doing! Now you shall be poor, and also by wrong-doing! Well – which is it to be – prison – or one thousand pounds?'

'I haven't got one thousand pounds,' wailed Winkle. 'I've only seven hundred in my long red stocking at home.'

'Bring me that,' said the gnome. 'And work hard and honestly for the rest, which you must bring to me as you earn it. And remember this, Winkle – riches got by ill means will sooner or later fly away, even as yours have done! Now go!'

Winkle stumbled home, sobbing and crying, to fetch his hoard of money. He was bitterly ashamed of himself. His neighbours pointed at him and nodded their heads.

'We told him so!' they whispered to one another. 'Meanness and dishonesty only come to one end!'

Poor Winkle! He is working hard every day now. His hoard of money is gone, and he is trying to earn more to make up the thousand pounds. But he has learnt his lesson. If he borrows, he pays back. If he finds what isn't his, he gives it back to the owner at once. He doesn't cheat, he doesn't shirk. And it may be that by the time he has earned enough money to pay the thousand pounds, he will be a different person – straight, honest and true.

I hope so, don't you?

13

What a surprise!

Barry was very fond of birds, and every morning he put out crumbs for them, and a saucer of fresh water. He made a bird-table, too – just a piece of wood on the top of a pole – and from it he hung strings of unshelled peanuts which he had carefully threaded together, and a coconut with a hole made at each end. He put all kinds of titbits on the table, and you should have seen the birds that came to visit it!

When Barry's birthday came, the postman knocked at the door and left three parcels, a small one and two big ones. Inside the small one was a silver pencil – and inside the two big ones were wooden nesting-boxes to put up in the garden for the birds to nest in! Barry was so pleased.

'Just what I've always wanted!' he said, looking at the two boxes in delight. They were very nicely made, and the top part, which made a slanting roof, could be lifted up – so that Barry would be able to peep inside and see if any bird had begun to nest there.

'I shall put these nesting-boxes up this very day,' said the little boy. 'I shall put one in the chestnut tree – I know a fine place there – and one I shall fasten among the rose-ramblers. There is such a small hole in each for the birds to get in and out that I am sure only the tiny tits will make their homes there. What fun it will be!'

So out he went very happily into the garden, and soon the two nesting-boxes were in their places. One was well hidden among the ramblers and the other was neatly hung on the trunk of a small chestnut tree, protected by an overhanging branch.

'If I were you, Barry,' said his mother, 'I would hang up bits of fat or peanuts near your new nesting boxes, and then, when the tits come to them, they will see the boxes, and perhaps think they are good nesting-places.'

So Barry hung up a few peanuts by each box, and a piece of suet too. In ten minutes' time the tits had found the nuts and the suet, and were very busily pecking away at them. Barry could hear them calling to one another in excitement.

'This is suet, this is, this is suet, this is! Peanuts, peanuts, peanuts! This is suet!'

The tits were pleased to find more food in the garden. They thought that Barry was the nicest, kindest boy in the world, and they were always happy in his garden. One of them flew to the top of a nesting-box. He wondered what it was – it hadn't been there before. He hopped about all over it, sometimes the right way up, sometimes upside down. He didn't really mind whether he swung one way or another!

Then he called to his wife, 'Come and see!'

She flew down to him. 'Look!' said the tit in excitement. 'There is a little hole here. It leads into a nice dark room. Let us go inside and see whether it would be a good place to nest in.'

So in they went, and they both decided that it would be exactly right. This was the box that Barry had put in the rose-ramblers. The other box was taken by another pair of excited tits, who were most delighted to find such a fine nesting-place.

'It's near plenty of food!' they sang. 'It's in the garden of the nicest boy in the world! There are no cats! We shall be safe, safe, safe!'

Then they began to build their cosy nests. They made them of the softest things they could find – bits of moss taken from the ditch, a great many hairs from the post against which the brown horses in the field rubbed themselves each day! And some hairs from the dog next door. When he shook himself a few hairs flew from his coat, and the tits were always on the watch for these. They would hunt about the lawn for them.

Then they lined their nests with soft feathers. Some they found in the hen-yard, and how they squabbled with the sparrows over them! The sparrows liked the feathers too, to make a lining for their nests, and tried their best to take them all – but the tits pounced down in a trice, and carried off most of the downy feathers under the very beaks of the angry sparrows!

The nest of the tits in the rose-rambler box was finished first. It was so cosy and warm. Barry knew that they were building there, for he watched them carrying moss and hair in their beaks to the ramblers. He was delighted. One day, when he knew that both the tits had left the nest, he went quietly to it and lifted up the roof-lid. He gazed inside before he shut down the lid, and to his great delight saw five pretty little eggs. Now there would be crowds of fluffy yellow baby tits calling all over the garden to their parents!

He ran indoors to tell his mother.

'I'm so glad,' she said. 'But if I were you, Barry, I wouldn't peep inside any more. The tits may not like it, and it would be so dreadful if you made them desert their nest and leave their eggs or young ones. It does sometimes happen, you know.'

So Barry did not go and peep for a long while. When he did the next time he got a great surprise, as you will hear.

Now, as you probably know, all birds and animals can see the little folk, although very few of us humans can do so. The tits especially are friendly with them, for the fairies love the merry, pretty little birds, with their bright voices and amusing ways.

Very often the tits went to the woods nearby where many elves lived, and in their hunt for small insects they came across many of the little

113

folk and talked to them. And one day the tits that nested in the rose-rambler box found an elf of great use to them.

She lived in a hole at the foot of an old oak tree. The two tits often went to hunt for insects in the bark and the elf liked their merry voices, and always popped her little golden head out to wish them good day.

One morning the tits were hunting in the oak tree bark when a gun went off not far away. It was the farmer shooting rabbits. It frightened the tits so much that they rose straight up into the air to fly – and one of them flew full-tilt into the branch overhead and hurt himself so badly. that he fell down to the ground in a faint, his eyes closed, and his wings drooping.

'What's the matter, what's the matter?' called his little wife, in a fright. She flew down to her mate, but he did not move. Then she heard a scampering of feet not far off and saw the bright-eyed weasel, whom all small creatures and birds fear, for he feasts on them.

'Help! Help!' cried the little tit, in a panic, and she flew up into the air. The weasel stopped – and then came running over to the oak tree.

But before he could snap up the poor little tit someone came rushing out of the roots of the oak. It was the golden-headed elf. She caught up the tiny tit and ran back with him into her home. He was safe there, for the weasel could not possibly squeeze into the small hole where she lived.

'I'll pay you out for that!' he shouted at her and ran off, mad with rage, for he was hungry.

In a few minutes the tit opened his eyes and stretched his wings, none the worse for his bump. When he found the elf bending over him, and heard what had happened, he was very grateful indeed.

'It is most kind of you!' he said, in his shrill little voice. 'Most kind indeed! Let me know, elf, if you want help yourself at any time, and my wife and I will be very pleased to do whatever we can for you!'

Then off he flew with his wife, back to his nest in the box, where he rested all day and was soon quite himself again. When their eggs hatched out into five pretty little youngsters, the two tits were mad with delight. They sang about them until everyone in the garden was quite tired of hearing how beautiful and how marvellous the baby tits were. But indeed they really *were* very sweet, for they were just bundles of blue and yellow fluff.

One day the robin brought a message to the two tits.

'Blue-tits!' he sang, 'I bring a message to you from the elf in the woods. She is very unhappy and bids you go to her.'

Off went the tits at once. The elf was not in her usual place under the oak tree – but they found her shivering in the ditch not far away, with only a cobweb shawl wrapped round her.

'What is wrong?' cried the tits, flying down beside her.

'Oh, little friends,' said the elf, 'a dreadful thing has happened to me. The weasel was so angry because I saved the life of one of you the other day that he vowed to force me to go away. He sent an army of red ants into my cosy home and they ate up all my pretty clothes, and bit me so hard that I could not stay there any more. Now they are building their nest in the oak tree roots, so I have no home. I don't know where to go, because if I choose another hole the ants will come after me there too. Now, here I am, cold and hungry in this ditch, with only this cobweb shawl to keep me warm. I am so dreadfully afraid that the weasel will come after me.'

'You poor little thing!' cried the tits, cuddling close to her. 'What can we do for you? Let us think hard!'

So they thought very hard, and then the little hen tit cried out in delight.

'I know! I know! Let the elf come to live with us in our nesting-box! It is true that we are rather crowded now that we have five babies – but it is warm and cosy, and the elf will have

116

plenty of company and be quite safe from the weasel there!'

'Oh, that would be wonderful!' said the elf, tears of joy coming into her eyes. 'Oh, there is nothing in the world that I would like better! I could look after the babies for you when you went out together, couldn't I!'

'Yes, you could!' cried both tits, delighted. 'There is one of our children who is far too bold. We are afraid he will climb out of the little entrance hole one day and fall to the ground. Then the weasel will be sure to get him. If *you* were living in the nest with us we should never be afraid of leaving the babies alone. Do come!'

The elf spread her pretty, gleaming wings, and flew up into the air with the tits. The weasel, who was hiding in the bushes not far off, gave a snicker of rage. He had been hoping to pounce on the elf that very day.

The tits took the elf to their nesting-box. She was just too big to squeeze in through the little hole, so she had to lift up the roof and get in that way. She cuddled down among the fluffy babies and was soon as warm as toast.

How happy she was there! And how pleased all the seven tits were to have her! She was so good to them all. She looked after the five babies carefully when the two parents were away, and wouldn't let the bold one try to climb out of the hole. She saw that each baby had his share of the food in turn, and would not let the strong ones rob the weak ones. She brushed their feathers and told them tales. They loved her very much indeed.

She was very warm and cosy there, and had plenty to eat, for the little tits brought her all kinds of food each day. They knew which flowers had the sweetest honey, and they were very clever at bringing leaves with dewdrops on them, so that the elf could drink. Nobody knew that the elf lived in the box, not even the other tits. It was a secret.

And then somebody found out. Guess who it was! Yes, it was Barry. He did so badly want to see how many baby birds the tits had in the rose-rambler box. So one sunny morning he tiptoed to it, after he had seen the two big tits fly out, and he lifted up the roof-lid to see inside.

He looked down – and there, looking up at him were five fluffy yellow baby-tits – and one pretty, golden-headed elf! She was cuddled down among the tits, her arms round them, the prettiest sight you could imagine!

Barry was so surprised that he simply stood and stared. Then he quietly shut down the lid and went away. It was the greatest and loveliest surprise of his life – a real secret that he couldn't tell anyone at all.

When the big tits came back, the elf told them what had happened. She was frightened. 'I must fly off!' she said. 'That boy will come back and take me away.'

'No, no,' sang the tits at once. 'Don't be afraid of Barry. He is the nicest boy in the world! He would not harm us, and he will not harm you. You are quite safe here. Let him peep at you if he wants to. He will never, never hurt you!'

When the five baby tits flew away into the garden in the bright summer-time, the elf stayed in the nesting-box and made it her home. She tidied it up, and she made a small cupboard for herself and a shelf where she put all her belongings.

'Do come back and nest here next year,' she begged the tits, who often came and peeped in at the hole to talk to her.

'We will!' they promised. 'We certainly will!'

So there the elf still lives, as Barry knows very well! He peeps at her once a week, and she knows him well now and smiles gaily at him. He has never told anyone his great secret – but I know because the tits told the robin and he sang it all to me! And how I'd love to go and peep in that box – wouldn't you?

More Beaver Books

On the following pages you will find some other exciting Beaver Books to look out for in your local bookshop

BEAVER STORY COLLECTIONS

If you have enjoyed all the stories in this book, why don't you try some more Beaver story collections, which are packed with funny, spooky or thrilling tales. They are available in bookshops or they can be ordered directly from us. Just complete the form below and send the right amount of money and the books will be sent to you at home.

☐ MY FAVOURITE ANIMAL STORIES	Gerald Durrell	£1.95
☐ MRS PEPPERPOT'S OUTING	Alf Proysen	£1.99
☐ GHOSTLY LAUGHTER	Barbara Ireson (editor)	£1.50
☐ GHOSTLY AND GHASTLY	Barbara Ireson (editor)	£1.95
☐ A BOOK OF BEARS	David McKee and Rosemary Debnam	£1.00
☐ A BOOK OF PIG TALES	David McKee and Rosemary Debnam	£1.25
☐ A BOOK OF ELEPHANTS	Katie Wales and David McKee	£1.25

If you would like to order books, please send this form, and the money due to:
ARROW BOOKS, BOOKSERVICE BY POST, PO BOX 29, DOUGLAS, ISLE OF MAN, BRITISH ISLES. Please enclose a cheque or postal order made out to Arrow Books Ltd for the amount due including 22p per book for postage and packing both for orders within the UK and for overseas orders.

NAME ....

ADDRESS ....

....

Please print clearly.

BEAVER BOOKS FOR YOUNGER READERS

Have you heard about all the exciting stories available in Beaver? You can buy them in bookstores or they can be ordered directly from us. Just complete the form below and send the right amount of money and the books will be sent to you at home.

☐ THE BIRTHDAY KITTEN	Enid Blyton	£1.50
☐ THE WISHING-CHAIR AGAIN	Enid Blyton	£1.99
☐ THE STRANGE HOUSE	Raymond Briggs	£1.25
☐ MR BROWSER AND THE MINI METEORITES	Philip Curtis	£1.50
☐ CREEPY CRAWLY STORIES	Barbara Ireson	£1.95
☐ SOMETHING NEW FOR A BEAR TO DO	Shirley Isherwood	£1.95
☐ REBECCA'S WORLD	Terry Nation	£1.99
☐ CONRAD	Christine Nostlinger	£1.50
☐ FENELLA FANG	Ritchie Perry	£1.95
☐ MRS PEPPERPOT'S OUTING	Alf Prøysen	£1.95
☐ THE WORST KIDS IN THE WORLD	Barbara Robinson	£1.75
☐ THE BUGBEAR	Catherine Storr	£0.95
☐ THE BARLEY SUGAR GHOST	Hazel Townson	£1.50
☐ PILKIE'S PROGRESS	Hazel Townson	£1.95
☐ THE ADVENTURES OF THE GINGERBREAD MAN	Elizabeth Walker	£1.50

If you would like to order books, please send this form, and the money due to:
ARROW BOOKS, BOOKSERVICE BY POST, PO BOX 29, DOUGLAS, ISLE OF MAN, BRITISH ISLES. Please enclose a cheque or postal order made out to Arrow Books Ltd for the amount due including 22p per book for postage and packing both for orders within the UK and for overseas orders.

NAME . . . .

ADDRESS . . . .

. . . .

Please print clearly.

BEAVER BESTSELLERS

You'll find books for everyone to enjoy from Beaver's bestselling range—there are hilarious joke books, gripping reads, wonderful stories, exciting poems and fun activity books. They are available in bookshops or they can be ordered directly from us. Just complete the form below and send the right amount of money and the books will be sent to you at home.

☐ THE ADVENTURES OF KING ROLLO	David McKee	£2.50
☐ MR PINK-WHISTLE STORIES	Enid Blyton	£1.95
☐ THE MAGIC FARAWAY TREE	Enid Blyton	£1.95
☐ REDWALL	Brian Jacques	£2.95
☐ STRANGERS IN THE HOUSE	Joan Lingard	£1.95
☐ THE RAM OF SWEETRIVER	Colin Dann	£1.99
☐ BAD BOYES	Jim and Duncan Eldridge	£1.95
☐ MY NAME, MY POEM	Jennifer and Graeme Curry	£1.95
☐ THE VAMPIRE JOKE BOOK	Peter Eldin	£1.50
☐ THE ELEPHANT JOKE BOOK	Katie Wales	£1.50
☐ THE REVENGE OF THE BRAIN SHARPENERS	Philip Curtis	£1.50
☐ FENELLA FANG	Ritchie Perry	£1.95
☐ SOMETHING NEW FOR A BEAR TO DO	Shirley Isherwood	£1.95
☐ THE CRIMSON CRESCENT	Hazel Townson	£1.50
☐ CRAZY SEWING	Juliet Bawden	£2.25

If you would like to order books, please send this form, and the money due to:
ARROW BOOKS, BOOKSERVICE BY POST, PO BOX 29, DOUGLAS, ISLE OF MAN, BRITISH ISLES. Please enclose a cheque or postal order made out to Arrow Books Ltd for the amount due including 22p per book for postage and packing both for orders within the UK and for overseas orders.

NAME . . . .

ADDRESS . . . .

. . . .

Please print clearly.